The Cowboy and His Christmas Rockstar

Cowboys of Rock Springs, Texas #5

Kaci M. Rose

Five Little Roses Publishing

Copyright

Editing By: Debbe @ **On the Page, Author and PA Services**

Proofread By: Nikki @ **Southern Sweetheart Services**

Blurb

The cowboy who just took over his parent's ranch. The rockstar who's trying to lay low after a recent scandal. And a little small town match making.

One well placed photo and a lot of lies send me running to my sisters in the small town of Rock Springs, Texas to hide from the press for Christmas.

Too bad my sister's plan includes the blind date from hell.

But my brother in law's best friend comes to my rescue.

Ford is every bit the hard muscle cowboy.

Next thing I know he's at my side for everything from the town's secret Santa and Christmas shopping to the Winter Carnival.

It has to be my sister's doing.

But when another record label calls me to talk via a little Christmas Magic the clock starts ticking.

Ford might be fine going with me to Nashville for a weekend but how will we survive a rock star's schedule of tours, recording, and PR?

Then the real reason comes to light as to why I was used staged on those photos and it's a doozy.

Santa do you have one last miracle for me?

Dedication

To the coffee that kept me going, and the kids that call me mommy.

Contents

Get Free Books!

Would you like some free cowboy books?
If you join Kaci M. Rose's Newsletter you get books and bonus epilogues free!

Join Kaci M. Rose's newsletter and get your free books!
https://www.kacirose.com/KMR-Newsletter

Now on to the story!

Chapter 1
Savannah

I used to think being on tour with a band was this glamorous thing. Shows in the evening, party all night, sleep in, wake-up, and then repeat in a new town.

Boy, was I wrong.

A cramped tour bus with a bunch of smelly guys, early mornings, and late nights. I cried in relief when we pulled into Atlanta for a few days and was able to get my own hotel room.

Even though we are in the same town for several nights, we still have press events, concerts, and appearances. In short, there's no downtime. It's all become such a blur.

The only thing keeping me sane is the lead singer's wife. She and I have bonded with the drummer's wife, being the only women on the tour.

I don't get to hang out with them as much as I'd like, since I'm the opening act. I'm always busy with the sound checks, and all the same events their husbands have to do, but it's still nice not being the only girl on the tour.

I thought things would be quiet in the hotel. I'm on a different floor than the rest of the band and was looking forward to some peace and quiet. So, I'm not sure who is pounding on my door at the ass crack of dawn, but I do know they must have a death wish.

I roll out of bed, still in my clothes from last night, because I was too exhausted to change. A quick glance in the mirror above the dresser shows my hair is mostly in place, but my make-up isn't. I rub at it, trying to fix what I can.

"Savannah, open up. It's Hal!" My manager yells.

What the hell does he want? I check the time, and it's just before eight in the morning, and my first event today isn't until noon.

I open the door and turn back to the mirror, attempting to fix my make up some more.

"I had a morning to sleep in, so what's so important?" I ask.

"Have you seen this?" He tosses his tablet on my bed.

"Hal, I'm still in the same clothes as last night. Which means, I came to my room and passed out on the bed, and you just woke me up, so what do you think?"

"You better take a look."

He nods towards the tablet. Taking a deep breath, I walk over to the bed and sit down. I look at the site he has pulled up. It's a gossip tabloid known for spreading lies and causing drama. In short, no one with any sense believes them.

"Why are you even looking at this site? When was the last time they reported anything that was true?" I ask.

"I don't know, but they were the first to report that article, and other more reputable sites have now reposted it, so read it."

As I scroll down, the headline makes me want to laugh. Anyone who knows the band wouldn't even give it a second look.

'Lead singer of the band 3 Stevens cheating on his wife?'

"Come on, we both know he's beyond faithful to her. Whoever they paired him with..."

"Look at the photo." Hal interrupts me with a tone I rarely hear.

Scrolling down some more, there's a picture of Steven, the lead singer, and me. The angle was taken very oddly, and it looks like we were leaving the club together last night. What you can't see is his wife, who walked out of the club behind us.

The pictures look bad because we're looking at each other and laughing.

"I remember this. We left the club and were laughing at the bouncer, who had just stumbled all over himself when some model started flirting with him. We were joking about how he must have been new. His wife came out of the club just behind us."

"Yet, she isn't in the photo. But you are making love eyes at him."

"What the hell are love eyes?"

"Those eyes you have in this picture where you're looking at him. The human equivalent of the emoji with heart eyes."

"You mean the eyes I have, when I laugh, and when I'm drunk and relieved to be leaving the club. The three of us shared a car back to this hotel, and they went to their room, and I came to mine."

"But that's not what they're reporting. His wife's phone has been blowing up by everyone she knows, and she's pissed."

"What? I'll talk to her. We were having a great time last night."

"She doesn't want to talk to you. In this business, appearance is everything. It looks like he's having an affair with the opening act, which is bad press for her and the band. They have already decided you should take the next several stops off and let all this die down."

"What? What do you mean take them off?"

"Go home for the holidays, stay out of the press, and let me clean this up. They don't want this kind of press around the band, and they don't want you around right now."

"So, I miss all the Nashville stops, The Grand Ole Opry, the press events, and the Christmas concert in New York City?"

"Yes. They said they would reevaluate the tour after New Year's."

I sit there stunned. Though I may not be a fan of touring, these are some of the biggest shows that I'll be missing.

"This isn't fair. I did nothing wrong, and they know it!"

"What did or did not happen, doesn't matter. It's that you let yourself be put in a position to allow a story like this to go viral. Do you understand that it's everywhere?"

"So, fix it. That's your job." I grit out.

"I'm trying, but to do that, I need you to lay low. It's a few weeks, until Christmas. Go home, visit your parents or your sister, and relax. Sleep in or read a book. If you show you're willing to do what's best for the band, I know I can have you back by the New York City concert."

Hal doesn't give me time to say anything else. Instead, he simply walks out of the door, leaving me speechless.

I've essentially been banished from the tour because one of the paparazzi got a well angled picture of me and him.

This sucks!

Go home for Christmas. Well, my home is here just outside of Nashville, and I'm sure it's surrounded by paparazzi by now. My parents are on a trip to the Caribbean and won't be home, until a few days, before Christmas.

I guess I can head to Texas and visit with my sister. She lives in a small town with her husband on a ranch out of town. It's been almost a year since I've been to Rock Springs.

My sister, Lilly, and her husband, Mike, visited me on tour when we were in Dallas and again in Austin. But that was almost six months ago, so I guess it's time to pay them a visit.

I should call and give them a heads up, but they would call attention to me at the airport, and I need to draw as little recognition as possible. After I shower and get dressed, I pack up my bags and go straight to the Atlanta airport and buy the first available ticket to Dallas.

Thankfully, my flight leaves in less than an hour, and between the fact that I'm in jeans, a sweatshirt, no makeup, sunglasses, and a baseball cap, no one has recognized me.

I have gotten several looks from security, but I keep my head down, and no one seems to pay me any attention. As I sit in the corner, waiting on my flight, I read through the articles that are circulating.

One pulled older photos from the tour, trying to guess when the affair started, and if I was just friends with his wife to throw off suspicion.

I sleep through the flight, and thankfully, I don't have a layover. Once we land, I quickly grab my bags and go to rent a car.

That's where my luck runs out.

The girl at the rental counter gushes, "Oh, my gosh. You're Savannah Baron! I saw you open with the 3 Stevens when you were here in Dallas."

"Shh. Please, I don't want people to know I'm in town."

"Are you visiting a secret boyfriend?" She whispers, but then giggles, too.

I guess she hasn't seen the article, and I run with it.

"Yes. We met when I was on tour here." I hold a finger to my mouth, indicating it's a secret that I'm in town.

She nods and tries to hide her smile, as she starts punching away and gets me an SUV to rent.

"I can't believe you'll be here through New Year's."

"Well, I'll be in and out of town, so it's just easier to rent the car, until then."

She nods again and hands me my keys and paperwork. Thankfully, I'm able to get to my car with no one else noticing me. I punch in Lilly's address in the GPS and start the hour drive out of town.

While driving to Rock Springs, I try to figure out what to tell Lilly, because she will want to know, and I don't want to lie to her. I guess maybe telling her the truth about what happened and what Hal said would be the best.

She won't care that I'm visiting her. I know that. In fact, they will probably put me to work in the barn with the horses, which I'm completely fine doing. I find the barn work calming. Maybe, it's the repetition of it, or that the horses will listen to you talk and not ask a million questions. Or maybe, it's the fresh air, but I think a few days working in the barn is just what I need.

As I drive through Rock Springs, I can see the place hasn't changed much, other than all the Christmas decorations are out, and this year there's no snow on the ground, yet.

Last year, there was a big snowstorm, before Christmas, and everyone was snowed in. For the first time in over a decade, they had a white Christmas, and it was when Lilly fell in love with her now husband, Mike.

I hope to find a guy who treats me like Mike treats Lilly. He looks at her like she's his whole world. Heck, all the guys in Rock Springs do.

Lilly has made some friends here, and the guys treat their girls like they are the most important thing in the world.

When the cowboys in Rock Springs fall, they fall hard and fast.

Maybe one day, when I'm done with my own headline tour and have a nice cushion in my bank account that will last through my great grandkids, I'll have time to settle down and find me my own cowboy. But I've learned the hard way a relationship just isn't possible when you are on tour for nine months or more.

As I pull into Lilly's ranch, I smile. They bought this place last year and have been working to fix it up, but Lilly has never been happier.

No sooner do I close my car door than Lilly is on the front porch.

"Vanna! What are you doing here? Why didn't you call me? We would have picked you up at the airport!" She runs over and pulls me into one of those big hugs, only your older sister can manage to give you. It's a hug that promises everything is going to be okay.

That's when the wall breaks, and before I know it, I'm crying.

"I messed everything up," I wail.

"Oh, Vanna. I bet it's not as bad as you think. Come on inside and tell us what happened, and we will help you fix it," Lilly says.

"You bet we will," Mike says, as he grabs my bags for me.

I follow them into the house and collapse on the couch. Lilly hands me a cup of spiked eggnog before she and Mike sit down.

"Now, let's hear it. Then, we will figure out how to fix it."

This is exactly what I needed.

Chapter 2

Ford

I'm heading over to my buddy Mike's place to check out a horse. He takes in abandoned and abused horses.

Unfortunately, we have quite a bit of that happening around here lately, and they are overwhelmed with the horses they need to rehabilitate. So, I agreed to come over and take a look at one and possibly take it back to my ranch to help them out.

Recently, I took over my parents' ranch, and thanks to my sister who came in for a visit, the books are finally organized. So now, I feel ready to take on a new project and help Mike out.

Last month, he asked me to help, and I felt bad, but I just wasn't in a position to give him a hand. He understood, so now, I'm here to help.

As I pull up to his house, there's a strange car in the front yard. Lilly must have a visitor, so I head straight back to the barn and back up my trailer to the door to make loading easier.

Mike is there to greet me when I get out.

"Hey, man. I'm glad you made it. Lilly wants me to insist that you stay for lunch before we load up the horse," he says.

"You know I won't pass up a home cooked meal."

I follow him into the barn, and in the front stall, there's a large, dark brown horse.

"This is the stallion that was rescued in the sting operation at the church. The one Pastor Greg helped with. He needs some one-on-one attention. Since we aren't looking to do breeding here, and I know you have experience with it, I thought maybe he's a better fit for you."

"I'm shocked they didn't try to use him for breeding," I say.

This guy was part of what is thought to be an illegal rodeo that's dumping horses in town that are close to death. The cops are mystified as to why they're being dumped in Rock Springs, but also why they are left alive. Normally, they shoot them and leave them in a ditch somewhere.

They caught one of the guys in the sting. He was dropping this horse off, but unfortunately, they didn't get anything from him. Still, they could charge him with several cases of horse theft, so that's something at least.

As I check out the horse in front of me, he seems hesitant of me, of people in general, and it's no surprise. I can only imagine what he's been through. All the horses that have turned up have been starved, beaten, and drugged.

My dad taught me to look at the horse's eyes. He says you can tell all you need to know from their eyes. While my dad was much better at reading their eyes than I am, I will say this one has soft eyes.

Actually, his eyes remind me of my horseback at the ranch. He was a rescue as well. When this guy turns and looks at me, he holds eye contact, and I swear something passes between us.

"What's his name?" I ask.

"We haven't named him. We've been calling him Stallion. He doesn't match any of the missing horse reports on file. At least, not in this area. Miles and his guys haven't found anything. Though he has some unique markings on his chest, so if there was a report, it would be easy to match him."

Miles is the state trooper, who has been working the case and assigned to Rock Springs since this is where the horses have been dropped off. He's a good guy, and I kind of hope he sticks around after the case is over, because he fits in well around here.

"Well, I'd be happy to take him and see what I can do. How much?" I ask.

"Come on, Ford. You know what these guys have been through. I'm not charging you for him."

"I understand, but you're still running a business. He's cost you food and vet care. So, you need to get something for him. Plus, then there will be a bill of sale."

We go back and forth for a bit, and then finally, we agree on a price that I still think is half of what I should pay.

Mike goes on to show me a few of the other horses, and how they are doing. We stop at Snow White's stall. When they took her in, she was pregnant, and then delivered an all-white foal they named Peppermint.

I glance around the barn looking for Black Diamond, the first horse they rescued, and find a woman standing in front of her stall, petting her.

This woman isn't anyone I have seen before, so I look back at Mike.

"Who's that?" I nod towards Black Diamond's stall.

"That's Savannah, Lilly's sister. She surprised us yesterday and will be here through Christmas."

"Wasn't she the one on tour?" I ask, remembering Lilly talking about her.

"It's a long story, but it needs to stay on the down-low that she's here, okay?"

"Of course, man. Anything you need."

Mike's phone rings then, and he steps away to take the call, leaving me to watch Savannah. She looks relaxed in jeans and a loose sweater with her hair pulled back in a messy bun. Though she doesn't look like she has an ounce of make-up on, she's still stunningly beautiful.

Black Diamond seems to take right to her. While that horse has come a long way, she's still nervous with new people, so for her to take to Savannah, says a lot. I always believed horses were a good judge of character.

"She likes you, and she's picky," I say with a smile, as I walk over to them.

Savannah offers me a tense smile, so I try again.

"I'm Ford, and Mike's one of my best friends."

"I'm Savannah." She says more out of polite-ness than wanting to talk.

"Lilly's sister, right? I'm sure she's happy to have family around for the holiday. She said her parents were doing a Christmas cruise. I didn't even know that was a thing."

"Yeah, neither did we, but leave it to our par-ents to find something like that. They spend their winters in Arizona, so you would think that would be enough of an adventure."

"My parents just retired to Arizona as well. They love it there. They're in Tucson. I guess my dad likes being so close to Tombstone and learning about all the Wild West stuff."

"Once a cowboy, always a cowboy, huh?" She finally smiles at me.

"Yeah, that's never truer than it is out here. My mom had to talk him into finally handing the ranch over to me. It took her four years to convince him I was ready."

"I'm sure that will be Mike and Lilly when the day comes. But who knows? They both seem to just fit here like it's where they were supposed to be all along. Most people don't find that."

I get the feeling she's talking about herself, but I don't want to pry. While I know a little about her, we did just meet, and I'm sure she has no intentions of spilling her soul to some strange cowboy.

"Well, we should head up to lunch. Lilly insisted I stay, and I'm not one to turn down a home cooked meal. I don't get many of them now that my mom is gone."

"No wife to cook for you? I thought that was a prerequisite for owning a ranch around here."

"Seems like it. But no wife or girlfriend, either."

She laughs, as we walk back towards the house.

"Let me guess. Lilly and Riley have been set on trying to set you up? I've been here less than twenty-four hours, and they're already hinting at how I should meet this guy or that one."

Riley is Lilly's best friend, and the whole reason she's in Rock Springs, to begin with. It all started, when Lilly was a truck driver, and Riley was hitchhiking to run away from an abusive ex-boyfriend. Lilly was the one to pick her up and bring her here, where she met her now husband, Blaze.

"Oh, yeah," I say. "They get worse if I go too long without going on a date. I think they're so happy that they want everyone to be as happy as they are."

"I get that, but my sister doesn't take no for an answer. I'm on tour nine months out of the year, and it isn't easy on a relationship. Though, I would think she of all people would understand. When she was truck driving, she couldn't keep up a relationship, either."

"Yeah, it took a blizzard to snow her in for her to realize Mike was worth settling down for. That's how she tells that story to anyone who will listen, while Mike smiles, like she hung the moon, when she does," I laugh.

It's then that Lilly walks out of the back door and greets us.

"Come on, you two. Lunch is ready. I'm glad you could stay, Ford." She hugs me, as I step onto the porch.

"Of course. There's no way I'd miss your cooking."

As we sit at the table, I can see that Lilly has set us as couples. There are settings for two people on each side of the table, instead of spreading out with one person on each side. She insists on Savannah and me sitting next to each other.

When she goes back to the kitchen to grab the food, I lean over and whisper to Savannah.

"I smell a setup and apologize in advance for this," I tell her.

"When she said she'd invited you to lunch, I figured as much. And she wonders why I hesitate to visit often." Savannah has a soft smile on her lips, but a far off look in her eyes.

Mike and Lilly come out of the kitchen with lasagna and garlic bread.

"Ford, I made you a second lasagna for you to take home and freeze. Never hurts to have some freezer food," Lilly says.

"My sister was here earlier this month to help get the books back on track, and she filled my freezer, too. She said the same thing."

"How is your sister doing?" Lilly asks.

"Callie is good. Her husband was on some business trip when she came to visit."

"She hinted at being pregnant?" Lilly asks.

Callie and her husband, Jay, have been trying to have a baby for a few years, but it hasn't happened. She blames his crazy schedule. The company he works for opened a new branch, and he's been traveling between both places to get it set up.

When she can, Callie has been going on weekends to visit him, but I'm sure the stress hasn't helped. I guess, after the first of the year, things are supposed to calm down.

"No, I haven't heard anything. Jay is supposed to be done with the traveling sometime in January. Then, they plan to try again from what she told me when she was here."

"You'll be a great uncle. You can teach them to ride a horse, and when they get in trouble, you'll have free labor on the ranch," Mike laughs.

Lilly looks between me and Savannah, and I know whatever she's going to say next is well thought out.

"So, Mike, what did you think of Stallion?" She asks.

"I think I can work with him. He reminds me a lot of some horses my dad would bring in."

"Will you breed him?" She asks.

"I'm not sure who would want him, but I might see what he can do."

Lilly says to Savannah, "His dad bought a horse for cheap once, trying to help a guy out who was down on his luck. The horse turned out to be a champion racer. He's bred the horse a few times, and the foals sell for a pretty penny."

I never thought about getting into horse breeding, but my sister thinks that's the route we should take the ranch. The numbers don't lie either. The last foal from that horse sold, and the money covered the ranch expenses for almost a year.

"I still want to work cattle. The ranch has been a cattle ranch for three generations now. While I don't want to lose that, I can't lie. Horse breeding is hard to pass up, because of that income."

"It seems horse breeding would be easier than cattle?" Savannah asks.

And just like that, we launch into ranch talk, and she's able to keep her own and knows a lot more than I would have expected a singer to know.

Just goes to show that you shouldn't underestimate anyone. The more she's able to talk about ranch work, the more turned on I get.

As soon as lunch is over, I make my excuses and load up the horse to head home. I remind myself Savannah is only here for a few weeks and to not get attached.

In the back of my mind, I know I've already lost because Lilly always has a plan.

Chapter 3
Savannah

"Rise and shine, sleepyhead!" Lilly sing songs, as she dances into my room and opens my curtains.

The bright sunlight fills the room, and I turn over, putting my back to the window, and groan. I crack open one eye to look at the clock on my nightstand to see it's just after seven in the morning.

"One of the perks to being kicked off the tour was being able to sleep in," I groan.

"You did sleep in. Mike and I are up at five every morning, getting morning chores done."

"Sleeping in to someone on tour is noon."

"That's not going to happen around here. Half the day is gone, and farmers' and ranchers' hours are different. We live and die by the daylight. Let's go. I have breakfast for you." She says, smacking my butt, before leaving.

I groan, toss off the covers, and get ready because I know she won't let me go back to sleep. I make myself a mental note to get to bed earlier than one a.m. tonight. Trying to switch around my schedule, isn't as easy as I thought it would be.

When I walk into the living room, there are boxes everywhere. I almost trip over one on my way to the kitchen.

"Jesus, what's with all the boxes?" I ask, heading straight for the coffee.

Thankfully, Lilly knows better than to wake me up without any coffee made.

"We're setting up the Christmas decorations today. It's our first Christmas here, so we're going all out, especially since my sister will be here."

She smiles at me, and I can't be mad at her for being happy I'm here. So, we eat breakfast, and Lilly gives Mike and a few guys marching orders for decorating outside, and we start on the tree.

"I thought you would want a real Christmas tree," I say, pulling out the parts to put together the fake one.

"I do, but it's too early to set up a real one, so we'll set up this fake one, and then get a smaller real one to decorate closer to Christmas."

"You're crazy," I shake my head.

"Christmas is our holiday. It's when Mike and I fell in love and got married. We'll always go over the top, even if it's just the two of us."

"I'm really happy for you two. You are so much happier since you met him. I hope to find that one day, maybe."

There's a slight pause, and I take this time to look over Lilly. Her brown hair that matches mine is pulled back in a ponytail, and she's in a flannel shirt and jeans that hug her curves.

Growing up, she was always more of a tomboy, but the rancher wife look suits her. She is much more herself.

"Listen, I looked up the articles online about what's being said about you. That reporter was at the perfect angle and snapped a photo at the exact right time."

"I know. I was friends with the guy's wife, and I have no idea why she turned on me like this. My manager says it was all her, pushing me off the tour. I just don't get it."

"Honestly, I don't know her, but if her husband made the wrong comment about you, she could have let her jealously get in the way. Have you thought that it might have nothing to do with you? Maybe, he really is cheating, but not with you, and she just thinks it's with you. Who knows?"

"I swear it's all worse than politics." I groan and finish setting up the tree.

"What are you going to do next?" Lilly asks.

"Well, my manager mentioned lying low, until New Year's, which sucks, because some of our biggest shows to date are coming up. But I may not have a choice."

"Well, you're welcome here for as long as you need, no matter if it's a week, a month, or a year. This will always be home for you."

This is why I need more family around me. The loyalty and love are something I miss on tour.

Reaching over, I pull my sister in for a hug. I have missed her so much more than I realized. While this time out from the tour sucks, I am grateful to be able to spend some more time with her.

Neither of us says anything, as we start on the lights for the tree.

"I was thinking of inviting Mom and Dad out here for Christmas. Their cruise gets back a few days, before Christmas, and that way they don't have to try and plan anything. With you here, I think it just makes sense," Lilly says.

"I'd like that. Though, I'm surprised Riley and Blaze aren't having a big get together at their place."

I love Riley and Blaze's love story. When Blaze found Riley, he knew she was his, and he wouldn't let her go. Blaze's family protected her when her ex came after her. When life settled down, Riley reached out to Lilly later to thank her, and they had dinner and have been best friends ever since.

In fact, it was Riley that Lilly was visiting, when she got snowed in here last year. That led to her meeting Mike, and they were married by the new year.

Sometimes in your life, some people are just meant to be there, and you don't see the whole picture as to why, until many years down the road. That's Riley and Lilly for sure. Anyone here would agree.

"Oh, they are on for Christmas Day. Blaze's parents are doing their annual Christmas party the week before. So, we're doing Christmas Eve here. I need to find out if Ford plans to have his family visit because if he's going to be alone, I want to invite him over."

"My guess is the event on Christmas Day isn't going to be small, either?"

"Just family and a few close friends. But yeah, that means Blaze's siblings and their spouses, which makes five couples and two kids. Then, Ella's parents, her brother, sister, and their spouses, plus her brother-in-law. The five of us, plus Pastor Greg and his wife, Abby. Possibly Ford. Plus, I think Hunter and Nick's parents as well, so close to thirty people."

"That family doesn't do anything small," I say, hanging an ornament and rolling my eyes.

"Well, when you have fourteen just between the siblings, their spouses, and kids, then you add in-laws, yeah it grows fast. It was overwhelming at first, but you get used to it. It's a lot of people who have your back when you need it. But when they get together to get something done, it gets finished fast. I wouldn't trade them for anything."

"I wish I had a group of people outside of you, Mom, and Dad that I trusted like that."

It's so hard to know who to trust on tour. So many people want to dig their claws in and ride the train to fame, or even get their fifteen minutes in. It's easier to just keep everyone out.

"You can have it too, Savannah. You're my sister, so that means they have your back. They will do anything for you, too. We'd love you to settle here, even just between tours."

"I wish. When I'm not touring, I'm recording music, and I have to be in Nashville."

"I know. This is just my way of saying I miss you and wish you were around more."

"I miss you, too. I really do love it here and wish I could spend more time here, but unless it's forced like this, I'm just not sure how."

Chapter 4

Ford

Even though my mom finally convinced my dad to retire from the ranch and hand it over to me, he still can't fully let go. That's why every Friday, he calls for an update on the ranch.

I don't mind, as it allows me to catch up with them, and I know he's always there to talk things over. Though this week, I'm not sure what he will say about the stallion I got from Mike. I still haven't given the horse a name and know I need, too.

It's always been the lady of the ranch, who names the new horses, and since I'm not married, the lady of the ranch is still my mother. So, I take a photo of Stallion, while he's out in the pen, and then send it to my parents.

Me: This guy is new and needs a name.

Dad: Can't wait to hear all about him. Will talk with you soon.

Mom: His coat is whiskey colored, so I think his name should be Whiskey.

Me: Whiskey it is. He was abused, so he needs a lot of extra love.

Mom: You will do great with him.

I keep watching Whiskey, as he moves around the pen and then stops to look at me.

"Well, Whiskey, it looks like you like it here. I'll give you the weekend to get acclimated to your new surroundings, but Monday morning, we start getting to know each other."

He nods his head and snorts like he understands everything I said. Who knows, maybe he does? I hope to gain his trust, but I want him to trust people in general again, too.

I also need to see how he does with other horses, because if he's going to be used as a stud horse, then he needs to be good around them. He has a long road ahead of him, but I think he's up for the challenge.

Heading into the house to my office, I get ready for my dad's weekly call. I pull up the books on the computer that my sister set up. Though I know my dad was hesitant about switching his way of doing things, but now appreciates it, because he can watch how things are going from wherever they are.

As I'm going through my emails, the phone rings, and I don't even check the caller ID.

"Hey, Dad."

"Wrong person, unless you know something I don't." My friend, Brice, chuckles.

"Sorry, just expecting my dad's weekly call any time now."

"I figured, but I wanted to see if you have dinner plans. I was thinking of picking something up at WJ's and bringing it over. It's been a while since we hung out. We have both been busy."

"Yeah, that's fine. You know what I like."

"Okay, see you in a few hours." He says and hangs up.

Brice is the town doctor, and we've been friends for a long time. While my mom home schooled me and my sister here on the ranch, she made sure we had friends.

My mom is friends with Brice's mom, so they were always over here having lunch on the weekends, and Brice and I would hang out in the barn or go riding with my dad.

Now, he's the town doctor and just as busy as any rancher. He also owns a small plot of land with a few animals as well.

When the phone rings this time, I check the caller ID, and sure enough, it's my dad.

"Hey, Dad," I answer.

"Son, let's talk about Whiskey."

I knew that was going to be the first thing he wanted to hear about because my mom is sitting right there and will be asking.

So, I go on and tell them about how he came to be at Mike's ranch, how Mike called, the price we landed on for him, and how I think I can work with him. We talk about his first few days here at the ranch, too.

"If you can earn his trust, he sounds like a solid horse," Dad says.

"I think so, too. There was something in his eyes. It reminded me of Phantom when we first got him."

Phantom is my horse and has been since we got him just before I turned sixteen. He was being sent to a slaughterhouse and had been abused and neglected for a while before my dad rescued him.

It took us a while to earn his trust, but he took to me first, and my dad said it was a sign he was meant to be mine. I worked with him all summer, and my mom gave me a break on schoolwork, saying learning to build trust in a horse is a lesson that will serve me for years to come.

I didn't understand it then, but I know now. Earning a horse's trust is a lot like earning a person's trust. You have to work at it and actually warrant it.

"Well, if that's the case, you know what to do, and how to gain his trust. What do you plan to do with him, once you do?" Dad asks.

"Well, if he's okay around other horses, I'd like to look at using him as a stud. He won't get much money, but I think he'll do okay. I know a few young guys here who are itching to get on the rodeo circuit, so I might see if we can up his value with some buckles, and then get one of them to ride him."

"Don't get any ideas of trying to enter him into some shows yourself to up his value!" Mom yells from the background.

"I never had any interest in rodeo, and I don't plan to start now. If anything, I'll find someone to ride him." I assure her, but I know she will still worry.

"What's going on in town?" Mom asks, wanting to stay current on town gossip.

I hesitate a moment. I would normally tell Mom and Dad that Lilly's sister is in town and that we had lunch together when I picked up Whiskey. But I know Savannah is trying to keep a low profile and the fewer people who know she's here the better.

Plus, my mom is good at picking up, when there's something more between me and a woman, and the fact that I haven't stopped thinking about Savannah would be something my mom would harp on.

I don't need to give her any more ammo than she already has. She's as bad as Lilly is with trying to set me up with someone. I know it's because she wants me to be as happy as she and dad are, but it doesn't help.

"I'm not sure, really. I was only off the ranch to pick up Whiskey at Mike and Lilly's this week. Brice is coming over for dinner, so he will know what I missed." I tell her.

"Well, you be sure to call me, if there's anything good. I don't want to be too far out of the loop when I talk to the ladies on Sunday."

The ladies are the church ladies and otherwise known as the town gossips. They know your business, talk and debate your business, and tell you about their opinions on it. They meet every Sunday at church, but also at the beauty shop, during the week.

They are also fiercely protective of people in town and don't take well to outsiders, so while they may know your business, they won't tell it to just anyone. At least, there's that.

Mom hasn't been able to completely step away from all things Rock Springs, since her move. She still talks with the girls every Sunday to keep up on what's going on.

We all talk some more about the ranch business, and how Lilly and Mike are doing, and plans for Whiskey, before we hang up. I'm able to finish going through my emails before Brice arrives.

"Ford?" He calls out.

Brice is one of those friends who doesn't knock now that I've taken over the ranch. He just walks right in and makes himself at home. So, when I come out of the office, he's already setting up the food at the table.

WJ's is the local bar in town that also has the best food around. Nick, the chef, has won many awards and could easily work in some fancy Dallas restaurants, but he grew up here in Rock Springs, and this is where he wants to live.

So, Jason, who owns WJ's, brought him in as a partner, and then opened the restaurant side. The place has been booming ever since and has even been featured on a few TV shows.

"Hey, great timing! Just finished the call with my dad," I tell him.

"Please, tell me you have something stronger than beer," Brice says, as he finishes setting up dinner.

"That kind of a week?" I ask, as I head to the kitchen and get the whiskey.

"Yes, it seems every kid decided to get stitches this week. Outside of my practice in medical school, I've never done so many stitches." He slumps in the chair across from me, as I pour him a drink.

"We have had our fair share of stitches, too. I'm sure you remember how stupid we used to be. We'd jump off things we shouldn't and jump into piles of things we shouldn't," I chuckle.

"Yeah, but it's worse now with social media. They see other kids posting videos of doing something, so then they try to copy it, and of course, fail miserably at it. I miss the days when the most fun was running around hay bales in the field. Now, they're doing all these stunts on tractors."

We take a few bites of food before he changes the subject.

"So, rumor is you got yourself a new horse?" I shake my head in disbelief about how he heard about it so fast.

Besides the beauty shop that Megan owns and the diner, Brice's office is the next place for town gossip. People talk as they're being treated.

I go on to tell him about how I came to get to the horse from Mike, but once again, leaving out anything about Savannah. Though, I know as soon as Brice knows about Savannah, I will have a ton of questions to answer. Questions I'm not ready for.

"What did your mom name him?"

I hold up my glass.

"Whiskey." I chuckle, as Brice shakes his head.

"Whiskey and Phantom. Sounds like a stunt team."

"I hope they get along. I'm not sure what I'll do if they don't."

"You are already attached to him, aren't you?" Brice asks and watches me, as I answer him.

"Yeah, there was something between us the day I saw him in Mike's barn. Like maybe he knew he could trust me. I plan to start working with him on Monday, so we will see."

"How are your parents doing?" He thankfully switches the subject.

"They're good. My mom is hoping you have some town gossip since I haven't been in town this week."

"Let's see. Mrs. Willow and some of the older church ladies are planning a trip to Vegas. I guess they are all upset she got to go for Nick and Maggie's bachelor and bachelorette party earlier this year."

"Oh, yes. We all know about that. The one where Anna Mae and Royce came back married."

Royce is Maggie's brother and is now married to Anna Mae. Royce had been trying to get Anna Mae to go out with him for a year, before the trip. When they woke up married one night after a lot of drinking in Vegas, they were the town gossip for a long time.

Things worked out for them, though. They're happily married and expecting their first kid.

"Oh, Anna Mae's brother, Jesse, moved to town a few weeks ago. He just got divorced, because his wife was cheating on him. He's staying with Anna Mae and Royce for the time being," Brice says.

"I knew that. He seems like a nice guy. We should get together with him sometime."

"I agree, though it might not be for a while. Anna Mae and Royce are having some work done on their house, getting it ready for the baby, and I guess there was some damage from the blizzard last year. They are heading out to Walker Lake, while the construction is being done."

Royce's other sister, Ella, married Jason, who owns WJ's. He's also Blaze's older brother. Their family has a lake house in Walker Lake, Texas, which is several hours north from here; closer to Amarillo. So, I assume that's where they will be staying.

"Makes sense. It's best Anna Mae isn't around the construction, while pregnant," I say.

"Yep," he agrees.

Then, he goes on to give me more gossip for my mom, regarding some of the other people in town. After some consideration, I decide I need to talk to someone.

"Okay, I'm going to tell you something, but this isn't something for the town gossip. You can't tell anyone."

"Of course, man. Friend code first, always." Brice says, sitting up straight in his seat.

I know I can trust him. He's one of my best friends and always has had my back. He doesn't spread gossip about those close to him, even if he will sit here and tell me what he's heard all week.

"When I went to Mike and Lilly's to check out Whiskey, Lilly's sister was there."

"Savannah? I thought she was on tour."

"Yeah, I'm not sure what happened, but she's here for a while and doesn't want people to know."

"I don't blame her," Brice says, studying me.

It doesn't take him long before he picks up on the real reason I need to talk to him.

"Something happen?" He asks.

"Not really. Lilly asked me to stay for lunch, which I did, and it was an obvious setup, but I don't know. She wasn't the rock star sister I pictured her. In fact, she was very down to earth. When I saw her in the barn, she was relaxed and calm, and Black Diamond took right to her."

"Ahhh, you like her?"

"I don't know. The girl that I had lunch with. Yeah, I like her, but I don't think that's the real her."

"You won't know unless you get to know her."

"I don't think that's such a great idea."

I don't know if I'm telling him or myself that. Either way, it really isn't a good idea.

Chapter 5

Savannah

Why did I agree to this? There's a lot I will do for my sister, but I think I should have put my foot down on a blind date.

I know she wants me to be happy, and I'm sure she's thinking this will take my mind off the tour and all that mess. I know her intentions are good, but as I walk into WJ's, I have this sudden urge to run.

Though, I don't mean just run out of WJ's but run across state lines kind of run. The only thing stopping me is thinking about the conversation I'd have with Lilly later.

Walking in, I take a look around WJ's. It hasn't changed much. Still the country bar you'd expect, but bigger now that they added more dining. There's a dance floor and a small stage where they have live music. What catches my eye, is the wall made of reclaimed barn wood and brands from the local ranches all burned into the wood.

The bar itself is pretty large and is the focal point of the place. Above the bar is an American flag made of beer cans. Jason is behind the bar tonight with a guy I don't know, but it makes me relax, seeing a friendly face.

When Jason sees me, he waves, and I wave back. Then, a cowboy at the counter turns to look at me. It's Ford.

My heart starts racing that he's here, and he looks so damn good in those wranglers, button-down shirts, cowboy hat, and boots. I haven't been able to stop thinking about him, since our lunch with Lilly and Mike.

Maybe, that's why I agreed to this date to try to get him out of my head. I look around for my date, who's a ranch hand at another ranch in town.

"Savannah?" A cowboy approaches me.

I give him a friendly smile. "Yes?"

"I'm Dennis." He says with a smile.

Ah, my date. I look him over, and he isn't too bad looking. Not really my normal type. A bit too skinny, like he hasn't been working on the ranch long, or he doesn't do much manual labor. But he's tan, and he's in wranglers and boots.

"Nice to meet you." I smile at him and let him lead me to a table, even though I'm not a fan of his hand on my lower back.

Ford seems to watch us the whole time, and I can feel his eyes on me. I sit facing the bar and give a quick lookup to confirm Ford is indeed turned in his chair to watch the rest of the room.

Dennis sits with his back to the bar across from me. Then, he says the one sentence that lets me know from the start this isn't going to work.

"Wow, you are beautiful. I've never been on a date with someone famous before." He runs his eyes over me again in a creepier way.

Trying not to cringe, but I fail because I don't like his eyes on me. Since I never know what to say to that comment, I just smile.

"I haven't been here in a while. Has Nick added anything new to the menu?" I ask.

"Who's Nick?" He says, looking confused.

"The chef here," I tell him and wonder how long this guy has been in town if he has no idea who Nick is.

"Nah, a place like this doesn't have a fancy chef. We are in the boonies, sweetheart," he chuckles.

I turn the menu to the back, where Nick's profile is, along with the awards and competitions he's won, and the TV shows WJ's has been featured in. Then, I set it on the table and tap my finger on it.

He looks at me and shock crosses his face.

"So, how long are you in town for?" I ask.

"I started at the ranch about a month ago."

"Is that when you came to town?" I ask since he conveniently avoided my question.

"Yeah, something like that."

Okay, mister shady. I shake my head and glace up, finding Ford still watching me. His face has no emotion on it, but it's clear his eyes are on me. I try to offer a friendly smile, but I get nothing back.

Dennis looks back behind him at the bar.

"See someone you know?" He asks.

"It's a small town, and I know quite a few people here. Jason, who owns part of the bar, is serving drinks. He's the brother of my sister's best friend's husband. At the bar, is my brother-in-law's best friend. Jason's sister, Megan, and her husband, Hunter, are on the dance floor, and then Brice, the town doctor, is at the table over there with a few other ranchers."

I know several other people, but decide I've made my point. Something in my gut is telling me to make sure I let him know I'm acquainted with people here, and that people here know me.

"Yeah, the big downside of small-towns like this." He turns back to his menu.

"Not a fan of small-towns?"

"Not one bit."

"Then, why move here?" I ask.

"I'm a ranch hand, and the ranches are in small-towns. Trust me, if I could find work in the city, I'd do so in a heartbeat."

Lilly, what the hell were you thinking?

Rubbing my temples, I study the menu. Nick has several new additions, so I decide to try one of them. But I haven't yet had a single item from him I haven't loved.

We place our orders, and Dennis goes on and on about the ranch where he works. It's mostly complaining. For someone so set on doing ranch work, he seems to have a complaint about every part of it.

Actually, he reminds me of a guy I had a few dates with last year. All he did was complain about his job. Come to find out, he was dating me, thinking I'd be a meal ticket or a sugar momma to him. I ended that really fast. I'm starting to get the same vibes here, too.

Over dinner, I glace up at Ford, and he's still watching me. When I'm not looking at the bar, I can feel his eyes on me. It's a welcoming feeling, unlike when Dennis runs his eyes over me.

"So, what famous people do you know?" He asks.

I know quite a few, but I'm not going to gossip about them, either.

"Not as many as you would think. If I'm not touring, I'm in the studio making music," I shrug.

"Man, it must be great to tour and see the country. Will you be doing an international tour?"

"None planned, and touring isn't exactly what you think. I don't get to go sightseeing. When I'm not on stage, I'm on a cramped bus."

"I'm sure it's not that bad." He says as he watches people on the dance floor.

"I'm sure it is," I mumble, cross my arms, and start to plan my exit strategy now that we are done eating.

I can't send my sister an SOS text, as she will insist I give this guy a chance. Since Jason is here, there's a good chance Ella is here, too. I could excuse myself to the bathroom and see if she's in the office. If so, I know she'll save me. But she's pregnant, so she could be at home sleeping.

Damn it, I look around, trying to see who I know here that can help. Megan and Hunter have left. There are a few faces I know that I've seen before, but don't know their names.

I guess I'll have to be blunt and bolt. Just as I turn back to Dennis, someone walks up to the table.

"Savannah, Lilly mentioned you'd be here." A deep voice washes over me.

I know that voice. I look up to find Ford, standing there looking at me.

"Sorry, buddy. We're in the middle of dinner-," Dennis says rather rudely.

"We're finished with dinner," I add, begging Ford with my eyes to save me.

"Lilly wanted me to make sure you took a look at the food planned for the winter carnival, while you were here. They're trying some new dishes, and they want your opinion. If you have a minute, the menu is in the office," Ford says.

Thank you, Ford! I could almost kiss him in relief right now.

"Oh, I almost forgot. Let me go check that out now." I turn to Dennis. "I will only be a few minutes."

"Well, hurry back. You owe me a dance still," he huffs.

Yeah, so not happening. I grab my bag and follow Ford to the office. As we pass the bar, Jason gives me a wink, so I know he's in on this, too.

As soon as we enter the office, Ford closes the door, and the music and noise from the bar muffle.

"Thank you so much. Lilly set up this date, and I don't know what she was thinking. The only way she could have picked a worse date was picking a murderer."

"Well, you don't want to go home too early. Lilly will know you ditched him."

"True, but I'm pretty sure this is the only place open this late."

"It is. Which is why Jason called Dennis's boss and had him call Dennis back to the ranch." He checks his phone. "Jason just texted that he left, and to tell you Dennis will call you."

"If Lilly gives him my number, I'll kill her in her sleep," I groan.

"Well now, maybe I can turn the night around. Would you dance with me?"

Chapter 6

Ford

Brice and I came to WJ's for dinner tonight, but he just got called away to the clinic, so I'm sitting at the bar, talking to Jason.

"Damn, I forgot Lilly said Savannah was coming here on a date tonight." He says in the middle of our conversation.

"What?" I ask to make sure that I heard him correctly.

"Lilly set Savannah up on some date with a ranch hand, and I'm supposed to watch out for her. She just got here." He nods and then waves at someone behind me.

I turn just in time to see Savannah wave back at Jason, and then her gaze lands on me. I don't offer her so much as a smile. She's here on a date with another man. Why does that bother me so much?

A man that I haven't seen before walks up to her and then guides her to a table. My skin crawls that he's even touching her. I've never felt this protective of someone before.

"Who is that she's with?" I ask Jason.

"Dennis. He's a new ranch hand. I don't know much about him, other than he works out at Chuck's ranch."

"The ranch behind yours?"

"Yeah. Chuck is a good guy, and he's picky on who he hires, so Dennis can't be all that bad."

"Right," I say, as Jason moves down the bar to serve drinks.

I can't take my eyes off Savannah. Even from here, I can tell she's already annoyed with the guy. I really wish I could tell what they are talking about. But when she points to Nick on the back of the menu and rubs her temples, I almost jump up from my chair right then, but Jason stops me.

"So, some big company in Dallas contacted me about wanting to franchise the bar," he says.

I take my eyes off of Savannah and look at him.

"I didn't know you were interested in expanding like that."

"I'm not really, but Nick said we should hear what they have to say."

"I agree with him."

"I guess they are sending someone out next month, after the holidays." Then, he nods to Savannah's table, "Doesn't look like the date is going so well, huh?"

"No, it doesn't." I agree, after turning to look at her.

"Well, we'll let them get through dinner, and then see how it goes," he says.

Once their food comes, it seems like Dennis does all the talking, and Savannah just has a blank look on her face. Once dinner is done, she starts looking around, like she's looking for someone to save her.

I flag Jason down and nod towards their table.

"I think she's had enough," I say.

"I agree. Listen, go remind her Lilly wanted her to look over the menus in the office for the winter carnival. I will text Chuck and get Dennis out of here. Then, I'll text you, when he's gone."

"Okay." I almost fly out of my seat and towards Savannah's table.

I waste no time getting there.

"Savannah, Lilly mentioned you'd be here," I say, getting her attention.

She looks up at me with relief and almost pleading in her eyes to be saved from this horrible date.

"Sorry, buddy. We are in the middle of dinner," Dennis says rudely.

"We are done with dinner," Savannah says, dismissing him.

While you're here, Lilly wanted me to make sure you took a look at the food planned for The Winter Carnival. Apparently, they're trying some new dishes, and they want to know what you think. The menu is in the office if you have a minute." Relief washes over her face at my words.

"Oh," she says. "I almost forgot. Let me go check that out right now." Then, turning to Dennis, she says, "I will only be a few minutes."

"Well, hurry back. You owe me a dance," he huffs.

That's not happening if I have anything to say about it. Savannah grabs her bag and follows me back towards the office. Jason gives her a wink, as we pass the bar, and I hide a smirk.

Once we enter the office, I close the door, happy to have her to myself for a few minutes.

"Thank you so much. Lilly set up this date, and I don't know what she was thinking. The only way she could have picked a worse date was picking a murderer." She says as she leans back against the wall.

"Well, you don't want to go home too early. Lilly will know you ditched him." I say, hoping to convince her to stick around, once Dennis is gone. I want some time with her tonight.

"True, but I'm pretty sure this is the only place open this late."

"It is. This is why Jason called Dennis's boss and had him call Dennis back to the ranch," I say, just as my phone goes off.

Jason: He's gone. He told me to tell Savannah he has a work emergency and will call her later.

"Jason just texted that he left, and Jason is to tell you Dennis will call you," I tell her

"If Lilly gives him my number, I'll kill her in her sleep," she groans.

I can completely agree with that.

"Well, maybe I can turn the night around. Would you dance with me?" I ask, hoping she will say yes.

She glances at her phone, and then back to me and smiles.

"I'd like that."

I swear my heart skips a beat right then and there. Holding out my hand, she takes it, as I open the door, and then lead her to the dance floor.

Jason watches with a smirk on his face, and I don't even try to hide the smile on mine. That is until we reach the dance floor, and I realize I hadn't thought this through.

Being this close to her, with my hands on her and her hands on me, is going to be heaven and hell all at once.

The moment her hand lands on my shoulder, my body shivers from her touch. If she feels it, she doesn't say anything. Though, when I place my hand on her waist, her entire body tenses. I take her other hand in mine and pull her close, but not close enough to touch. She doesn't need to feel that I'm already hard just from her touch.

I've never had a woman turn me on just from touching me like she is. As we start moving to the music, we both seem to relax into each other.

"Thank you for saving me tonight," she whispers.

"I didn't like you being near him. Something about the guy rubs me the wrong way."

"That makes two of us." She says, before resting her head on my shoulder.

Can she hear how fast my heart is racing? Does she know how hard I'm trying to keep my breathing even? Does she feel how hard I am?

I'm sure she can. Though, she doesn't seem to care, because she relaxes into me, as we move around the dance floor.

When the song changes into the next, and she keeps dancing with me, I decide to take the leap.

"Have dinner with me," I whisper against the top of her head.

She leans back and stares into my eyes. I almost wonder if she's even going to answer me before she finally speaks.

"I can't."

Well, that's not a no exactly.

"Why not?" I ask, wanting to know more.

"I will be going back on tour soon, and that won't be fair to you. Usually, I'm on the road more than I'm home."

"Then, why agree to the date with Dennis?"

"Lilly set it up, and I wanted to make her happy. She's been worried about me dating, since..."

I get a feeling there's something more than just the tour stopping her, and I need to know what it is because I want to help her.

"Since what?"

She takes a deep breath and gives me a shy smile.

"The last serious relationship I was in... was before I started focusing on my music, and it was... an abusive one. I got lucky and got help getting out."

We dance in silence for a bit, as what she says races through my head. I have this need to track down the guy who did this to her and give him a taste of his own medicine, but I know the last thing she needs right now is for my rage to take over.

"So, now Lilly is worried about you getting back out there?" I ask instead.

"Yeah. Since being in Nashville, I tried dating. I find most of the guys who are willing to put up with my crazy tour schedule are just trying to latch on for the fame or a free ride. So, I pretty much stopped dating. No good guy is going to put up with all this."

"The right guy will," I reassure her, but she just shakes her head.

"How is it fair to him? Have you seen the scandal that's all over the papers about me? If I was dating anyone, his face would be plastered all over the papers too about how I was cheating on him, even if I wasn't. One, that wouldn't be fair to him, and two, most people believe what they see on those websites, even if it's not true."

She's getting worked up, and that wasn't what I want. Instead, I pull her close to me again and hold her tightly.

"It's okay. I get it," I say in a soft tone.

She takes another deep breath and relaxes into me again.

"Besides, you are Mike's friend, and I don't want to make things awkward between us, when everything blows up in my face, as it always does."

I kiss the top of her head, and we just keep dancing. While I understand all of her reasons, my stupid heart still wants to try. It's yelling that there has to be a way to make this work.

Also, at that moment, I know what my mom said is true. Earning someone's trust is a lot like the lesson I learned from gaining Phantom's trust. Those lessons are going to come in handy now.

I need to take things slow, be patient, move at her pace, and show her she can trust me.

It's a good thing I'm good at being patient.

Chapter 7

Savannah

Lilly is just like our mom. She's sneaky and always has a plan. I'm now learning this the hard way. Maybe, I should have gotten a cabin in the middle of nowhere to hide in for the next few weeks.

I look around the living room, and I just know I'm not going to like whatever we are about to discuss.

Several church ladies are here, Abby, the pastor's wife, and Sage and Colt, along with Lilly, Mike, Nick, Ford, Ella, and her parents.

Thankfully, Lilly's living room is pretty large and connected to the dining room, so the overflow of people can still be in the conversation.

Abby stands with a big smile on her face.

"Thank you all for coming, though I'm sure it was more for Nick's food than for me, but I will take it!" She smiles, and everyone laughs.

Though, it's true. Nick brought some food he plans to serve at The Winter Carnival, and I know this is a meeting to wrap up all the loose ends because the carnival is next week.

Abby starts by going over the setup plans with Colt, Mike, Nick, and Ford. They have a bunch of guys ready to help set everything up and help break it back down after.

Then, she launches into plans for the Apple Pie Contest, the crafts booths, and the layout for the rides.

The entire time she talks, I can feel Ford's eyes on me. Every time I look his way, he gives me a smile that makes my stupid heart race. His brown eyes are soft, and he looks genuinely interested in helping with the carnival.

"Okay, one last thing, since everyone is here. I wanted to start a church fund to help new parents. I'd like to give each new parent a gift basket of essentials, some onesies, diapers, and that sort of thing. But above all, I'd like to build up the funds to offer financial relief for any parent who needs it."

Everyone starts whispering to the person next to them, and I feel a bit out of the loop.

"Abby, I know I'm not from here, so maybe it's not my business, but I get the feeling that you have someone in mind to help?" I ask.

She gives me a wobbly smile and nods.

"I was just at the birth of a young mom. Her husband left her, and she's struggling just to pay rent, much less buy stuff the baby needs.

She didn't even have a car seat. Greg and I paid for the basics for her from our own pockets, but we can't do that every time someone needs something."

I can only imagine how much they spent. We all know babies aren't cheap. One of the receptionists at the label had a baby last year, and I went to the baby shower. A nice dress for a little girl can cost almost thirty dollars, and they outgrow them every three months!

"I know how expensive it is providing for a baby. When buying a gift for the baby shower, I was shocked at how expensive everything was. The amount of stuff you need and what it costs is insane."

"You aren't joking," Ella says, rubbing her baby bump. Her due date was last week, and I know she's been miserable, and everyone has been on edge, waiting for her to go into labor.

Even though I want to help them, I know I should be laying low. I'm not sure if I should be drawing attention to where I am.

"Lilly, can I talk to you outside for a minute?" I ask.

She looks concerned, but nods and follows me out to the front porch.

"Everything okay?" She asks.

"I want to help."

"Well, I'm sure they could use some volunteers for set up."

I shake my head. "I know I'm supposed to keep a low profile, and any public appearance could mean the press swamping not just Rock Springs, but your ranch, too."

"Oh, Vanna. We don't care about that. There's a gate we have for security that you demanded we get after the horse was left on our property. We will be fine." She pulls me in for a hug.

"Are you sure? Because I'm thinking I want to offer to do a concert for them. It will do double duty. All the money from concert tickets can go to the fund, and then people will visit the carnival as well."

Lilly studies me, and I can't tell what her thoughts are. She's always been good at hiding them, when she wants, too.

"You miss singing, don't you?"

"Yeah, I was really excited for the Christmas stops, but now I won't be there for them. We were doing some benefit concerts, and I was looking forward to working with them, but this just feels different. The charities we were helping were big name charities. Not only is this something that really needs my help, but someone can really benefit from it."

Lilly smiles, "You're getting the small-town bug."

"What do you mean?"

"In this small-town, we help each other, and you get to see how your money and time can help someone else. It's more personal than giving money to some big charity and never knowing who or how it helps."

"But if I do this, it will pinpoint where I am. Paparazzi will likely swarm the town."

"Well, why don't you let the town decide what it wants? We dealt with it when Nick and Jason did the TV show for WJ's, so I'm willing to bet they are willing to put up with it now, too."

"But are you willing as well? The press will put it together that I'm staying here, and you will be hounded more than anyone."

"Of course, we are willing to deal with it. You act like it's a huge sacrifice for us. We have to put up with it for what a few weeks at most. You cope with them every day. If you can handle it, then so can we."

She hugs me again, and we head inside.

Entering the house, all eyes fall to me, as Lily says, "Hey, guys! Savannah had an idea, so she's going to explain it to you. But there would be a major pitfall to it, so she's going to leave it up to you, the town if we move forward."

"Okay, I'm sure by now it's no secret why I'm here for the holiday," I say and watch everyone guiltily nod their heads.

"Let me start by saying I didn't do what the tabloids are accusing me of. That being said, the moment they get a whiff that I'm in town, they will come in droves. It could be good for the carnival and all, but it has its downsides, too. They will hound anyone and everyone, trying to get you to talk about me, even if it's not true."

"Girl, you don't think we have dealt with them before?" Mrs. Willow says, and everyone agrees. "People came from all over, trying to get us to talk about Nick. Still do it every now and then. We don't talk to outsiders. It's just not our way."

"Okay, well, if I had stayed on the tour, we were going to do a few benefit concerts for some large charities. I was looking forward to helping, but being able to help here, just feels... different. I can't describe it, but I like knowing the people I'm helping."

"I told her she's getting the small-town bug," Lilly says and many of them laugh.

"Please, think this through, but if you are willing, I'd be happy to do a concert at the carnival. All the ticket sales could go to the fund for the parents, and also, the people coming in from out of town would more than likely spend the day at the carnival."

"It's a wonderful idea," Abby says. "We'll hold a vote at church tomorrow, and if it's a go, we can start making plans then."

"I'm happy to promote it with all my social media, and maybe, see if I can't get my manager to help do some radio promo in Dallas. I have a few friends at the record label that will share it, too. Just remember to tell the congregation that there's a big downside to the paparazzi knowing where I am."

"I promise to lay out all of the pros and cons," Abby says, as she writes faster than I thought possible on her clipboard. Many of the church ladies are on their phones. I'm sure already talking to people who aren't here.

When my eyes land on Ford, he has a real smile on his face, and something close to pride in his eyes. It's a bit unsettling, but I like that look on him, too.

As everyone starts moving around and eating food, Abby finds me.

"I really appreciate you being willing to do the concert no matter what the town votes," she says.

"Well," I say. "I love the idea of the town taking care of its own. It's been a long time since I've seen this sense of community. The music world is very cutthroat, and it's hard to know who to trust, and who has your back."

"That's why I love Rock Springs. We help each other, and it's like a big extended family."

"Lilly always keeps me up to date on what's going on in town. She said you were just married?" I ask.

A huge smile covers Abby's face, and a pink flush covers her cheeks.

"Yeah, last month. I wanted a small wedding, but the whole town showed up to show support for Greg. The help we got just planning the wedding was overwhelming. It was the first time I really got to see how far the town was willing to go for those it cares about."

"Did you guys go on a honeymoon?"

"Yes, we spent a week down in Galveston, Texas on the beach. Then, we enjoyed a few days in Houston, before coming back to start gearing up for The Winter Carnival." The smile never leaves her face, as she talks about it.

Here again, is yet another Rock Springs couple that found the true love I keep seeing. It gives me hope that it's out there for me, even if it's not right now.

As Ford walks up, Abby gives me a quick hug, before leaving us alone.

"So, I'm pretty sure the town is going to agree to the concert," he says.

"Why is that?"

"Because everyone in this room has said yes, and they have talked to at least two others already who all agree."

"News travels fast."

"Faster than you realize around here. So, that just leaves the fact that you need to go to the carnival to actually have fun and experience The Ferris Wheel view. I'm offering to take you, as a friend of course," he says.

My heart dips a little, when he friend zones himself, but it's better this way. I can spend a little time with him, experience the carnival, and have a good time.

"I haven't been to a carnival and actually been able to go on rides in a very long time, so I would like that."

"Oh, crap on a stick," Ella says from the kitchen.

"Everything okay?" Abby rushes to her side.

Abby is in school to be a midwife and is working with the local OBGYN doctors. Local meaning twenty minutes away. She has assisted at quite a few births already, and everyone has great things to say about her.

"My water just broke," Ella says, and sure enough, there's a small puddle of water on the tile floor at her feet.

As soon as everyone sees it, they jump into action.

"I'm calling Jason. He'll meet us at the hospital," Sage says.

"I'll call the rest of the family." Her husband, Colt, says, as they both head out of the front door. Probably, so they can hear when they make the calls.

"Come on, Ella Bear. Mom and I will drive you to the hospital." Ella's dad says.

"I'll come with you, too," Abby says, as they start moving her towards the door.

Nick says, "I will call Maggie and Royce." If I remember correctly, that's Ella's brother and sister.

If I know this town the way I think I do, then the whole town will know Ella is in labor within the next thirty minutes. While everyone is getting on the phone to someone, I just smile and head to the laundry room for the mop and bucket.

"Here, let me help," Ford says, as he takes the bucket to the kitchen and fills it with water.

I mop up the kitchen floor, and then he empties the dirty water for me.

"Oh, Savannah. You didn't need to do that." Lilly comes into the kitchen with the leftover food, now that everyone has left.

"It's okay. I didn't want anyone to slip and fall, and I really don't mind. You going to the hospital?" I ask.

Since Ella is Riley's sister-in-law, and I know how close Lilly is to that family, I'm thinking she really wants to go.

"Yeah, Mike and I are driving down as soon as we get the food taken care of."

"No, you are going now. I'll clean up this place. Go." I start pushing her out of the door.

"Are you sure?" Mike asks.

"Positive. It's the least I can do. Now go." I say, and Mike takes Lilly's hand and pulls her out of the door.

"I'll phone when we know something." She calls over her shoulder.

I turn and start putting food away and find Ford has beaten me to it.

"You don't have to do this. I got it," I say.

"If you weren't here, I'd be the one volunteering to clean up for them. So, I say we do it together. I've got the food. Why don't you start on collecting the empty cups and plates?"

I nod, and as we clean up, I find we work great as a team. In just over an hour, we have the house tidied up. Lilly calls, as we're taking out the trash.

"Hey," I answer on speakerphone, so Ford can hear.

"It's a boy! They named him Jason Junior, but plan to call him J.J. I'm going to text you a photo. Everyone says he looks just like Jason as a baby."

"Aw, that's so cute. I really thought she'd be in labor a lot longer," I say.

"So did we, but she had been having labor pains in her back, and she thought they were just false labor. By the time her water broke, she was pretty far along. They said she was ready to push right as she got to her room. It was a good thing that Jason beat us to the hospital."

"Give all three of them a hug for me and let her know I'd love to visit, once they are ready for company," I say.

"Same goes for me," Ford adds.

"Ford, you're still there?" Lilly asks.

"Yeah, I stayed and helped Savannah clean up. Actually, we just finished."

"That was really sweet of you. Can you make sure she eats dinner? We are going to grab something before we come home," Lilly says.

"I will make sure she eats," he smirks.

Lilly is getting sneakier and sneakier, and I need to step up my game to stay a step ahead of her.

Chapter 8
Ford

Looking out of my kitchen window, coffee in hand, I can't stop smiling. There's a light dusting of snow on the ground. Not even half an inch, but it's perfect timing since I'm taking Savannah to the carnival today.

This time last year, we were getting hit with a blizzard. One the state of Texas hadn't seen the likes of in over a decade. It made the whole town look like something from a postcard. It also kept everyone inside for a few weeks, but Pastor Greg still managed to put on the carnival, even if it was a bit later than normal.

Finishing up my coffee, I check on the ranch hands to see if they need anything this morning. I'm trying to stay busy because I feel like a kid in a candy store. While I love The Winter Carnival every year, this time I'm more excited, because I'm going with Savannah.

The town was overjoyed to have Savannah hold a concert, and tonight, I get to see her perform. Though I may have cheated and looked up a few videos online, and for sure, she's the real deal. Not only does she have a beautiful voice, but she has a stage presence that keeps you engaged the entire time.

I know I'm a bit biased, but I think her charisma and magnetism are stronger and more dynamic than the band that's headlining the tour. Part of me hopes they realize that soon and want her back because that's what she wants. But a larger part of me doesn't want her to go. It's apparent to me that the more time I have with her, the greater the chance I might get to be with her.

All morning, while we get the barn chores done, my mind is on Savannah. My ranch employs six ranch hands. Three are going to the carnival today, and the other three tomorrow. I like for them to go to big town events, but we can't leave the ranch unattended either.

These are all guys my dad hired, so I know they are good guys, and they prove it on days like today. Currently, they're all pitching in to get the chores done, so the ones heading to the carnival today can get on their way.

There isn't much to do on the ranch in winter, unlike in the summer. Around here, we are just tending to the horses, making sure the cows have enough to eat, and checking the fence line.

Between Thanksgiving and Christmas, I try to keep the workload low and give the guys a bit of a break from the rest of the year. Come January first, we start ranch inventory, before the spring, and that will take up all their time.

As the men head out to the carnival, I go back into the house and get ready. I don't want to get to Lilly and Mike's too early, but I don't want to be late either. When I say I will do something, I want Savannah to know she can count on me to do it.

As I pull up, Lilly and Mike are sitting on the front porch both with a big smile on their face that lets me know they're up to something.

"Well, don't you look handsome!" Lilly says as she gives me a hug. "I'll go let Savannah know you're here." Then, she disappears inside the house, leaving me alone with Mike on the porch.

"Savannah is my sister-in-law." He says as I sit down in the chair Lilly just left.

"Is that how it works? Thanks for clearing it up." I smirk at him.

"Her dad isn't here, so I'm giving you the talk. You know what Lilly means to me, and Savannah being her sister, means not even you are safe if you hurt that girl. She hasn't had it easy, but she's strong, and she's a fighter. You treat her better than you have ever treated anyone else, and we'll be okay."

"Of course, I know what Lilly means to you, and I don't take this lightly. Though, I'm aware Lilly is doing a little matchmaking. I'm not blind, but I promise you I wouldn't be going with her today if I wasn't serious."

Mike nods his head, acknowledging what I said and also effectively ending the conversation. We sit and enjoy the quiet for a moment before he asks about Whiskey, but the conversation is cut short when the girls come out onto the porch.

Savannah is in skintight jeans that show off every curve and an oversized sweater. Her brown hair and makeup are done up, and she has on a pair of cowgirl boots that match her sweater.

"Is it okay to keep this in your truck?" She holds up a large tote bag. "It's a few things I need to get ready before I go on stage."

"Of course." I stand and take the tote bag from her and offer her my other arm. "You ready to go?"

She takes my arm, and her gorgeous eyes light up with a bright smile. "Yep."

She says goodbye to Lilly and Mike, and I do the same. Though, Mike gives me the *'remember what we talked about stare.'*

I lead her to my truck, open the door for her, and then help her in. Then, placing the tote back in the back seat right behind her, I get in myself.

"You know I was here last year before the tour started, and I got to see this place covered in snow. I know that isn't normal, but I was kind of hoping it would happen again," she says.

How was she here last year, and I missed it? Of course, last year was when my dad was transferring everything over to me, and I had my nose buried in the ranch books. We were in and out of the bank, transferring documents and adding my name to things.

In fact, I was so engrossed in taking over, that I missed Mike and Lilly starting to date. When he called me to be his best man at the wedding, I was shocked. I didn't even know he'd met someone. I felt horrible and had him over for drinks and got the whole story.

"It changed the place for sure. I was in the process of taking over my parents' ranch, and my dad and I were doing a lot of the transfer stuff, so I didn't get to enjoy it as much as I wanted, too." I tell her.

I still can't believe she was here, and I missed her. Maybe, it's for the best, as she was just starting a new tour, and I wouldn't want to get in the way.

"So, what do you want to do first? Grab some food, walk around, and then save the rides for after your show?" I suggest.

"That sounds perfect. Oh, do you know where to park? There's a special performer parking that gets us close to the stage and also free parking." She begins directing me with the notes Pastor Greg gave her.

Greg and Abby are full of smiles, waiting there to greet us.

"You're early!" Greg says.

"I told you she would be," Abby says. "Savannah wants the full carnival experience." At Abby's words, the look Greg gives her, full of love, is the same one I see Mike give Lilly, and my dad gives my mom. It's the kind of relationship I want.

Before they start to let people in, they discuss times and a short soundcheck. Savannah takes it all in stride, and though I know she's used to this, before a show, watching her in action, is mesmerizing.

When she's done, she walks back over to me with a huge smile on her face. Then, we start walking to the section where all the food stands are.

"You miss it, don't you?" I ask.

"Yes, but not in the way you mean. I like singing and all, but I love helping people out and working with charities. The fact that I can do this for them is what has been really exciting. Yesterday, I sat down with Pastor Greg and Abby, and we went over the details, so we could talk about the concert. They had already sold all but twenty-five tickets to the show. In such a short amount of time, that's crazy."

I remember hearing them say they were going to have some VIP seating, but most of it was going to be standing room only. With that plan, they would be able to sell close to three hundred tickets.

"That's amazing! They'll be able to do so much with that money."

"Yes," she says. "Also, they're asking for donations at the gate, and at the entrance, and exit of the concert area. I'm hoping that me talking about it on stage will get people to donate more."

We walk the food aisle and end up with more food than I think we can eat. At least, that's what I thought until I watched Savannah. She may be small, but she can pack away food like my ranch hands do, and I'm impressed.

"My mom would love you. She likes a girl that isn't afraid to eat," I tell her.

"I'm going to gain so much weight here, but I don't even care. The food is so good, and it's real food. On the road, it's either fast food, whatever is cheapest, or whatever someone cooks, and there isn't a single person on that tour that can cook." She shivers, and I can only imagine the food.

As we start walking, she lets me take her hand, and I try not to make a big deal out of it, even if my heart is racing at the opportunity to even touch her.

"I'm guessing there wasn't much time to sneak away and try the local food," I say, ducking down a small walkway to avoid a man with a camera up ahead. If I can avoid it, I'm not going to let her be hounded by anyone today.

"Nope, we would get somewhere, do a sound-check, meet with our manager, and then, some kind of PR. It could be with a radio station, an interview, or a meet and greet. Then, we'd hurry back to get ready for the show, do the show, and sometimes an after party to be out and seen. Finally, we'd go back to the bus and crash. Then, we'd wake up in a new city and do it all over again."

"I know you like singing, but did you like doing the tour in that manner?"

She looks at me thoughtfully and smiles, but it's not a happy one.

"Honestly, no. There wasn't time to get out in the city, and to really spend time with fans. Actually, there wasn't time to do anything, really. Like I said, the food sucked, if we were even able to eat, and it was all work, all the time. Honestly, with that kind of pace, I understand why so many turn to drugs to try and keep up.

Even though I wouldn't, but I kind of get why someone might."

"Are all tours like that?"

"No, this is just the one my manager set up. Do you know the band Highway 55? Landon and Dallas? They took a stand, when they were touring, and wouldn't work with anyone on drugs, and slowed their tours down. It really changed things for the people working with them. Now, they have their own label, and they do things differently."

We spend the next hour walking around, and she gets stopped a few times with fans, asking for an autograph or a photo. I love taking those photos of her, but I stay in the shadows, watching her. She truly cares about her fans, and it shows in every interaction.

We are just finishing walking the art and crafts section when an alarm on her phone goes off. I'm shocked we made it this long without some paparazzi hounding us. Or maybe, they just got their shots from a distance, and I'm not realizing it.

"It's time to make our way back to the stage."

I walk with her back, and when she meets up with the sound guys, she turns to me.

"You can go meet up with everyone and come back for the concert."

"No way. I'm here with you, and I want to see you do what you do, soundcheck and all." I smile at her.

That seems to catch her off guard, and then she catches me by surprise when she leans in and gives me a soft kiss on the cheek.

"Go get a spot, front and center. It's the place during soundcheck. I'll be able to still see you."

Watching her go through the moves, during the soundcheck, and hearing her sing just for me, is different from the Savannah I saw on stage for the crowds.

Once the soundcheck is finished, she heads off to get ready. Then, they open the gates and people start filing in. I make my way to the side of the stage, and Abby flags me down.

"Savannah asked me to give you this." She hands me an envelope and inside are tickets to one of the VIP seats. Abby goes on with a huge smile, "She wants you to get the full experience-."

I shake my head and go find my seat. The buzz in the crowd is catching, and if you weren't pumped up before the show, you would be now.

It seems like forever, before the music starts up, and the show starts. I know this is a different kind of event for her, because she's the head-liner today, and she isn't opening for someone else. Everyone in the crowd is here to see her, and the pride that fills me isn't something I was expecting.

Watching her sing and feed off the crowd, has me mesmerized. She's even better to see in person than on the videos online. When she announces the last song, I start to make my way to the side of the stage. I want to be there when she's done and be one of the first to tell her what a great job she did.

As I watch her singing, she gives me a wink, before turning back to the crowd. The music scene has never really been my thing. Sure, I like to listen to music, but I can count the concerts I've been to in my life on one hand, but right now watching her, I know I could never get tired of it.

She wraps up the show and makes her way over to me.

"You were captivating," I say, as she wraps her arms around my neck, and my arms naturally go around her waist. She's leaning back, looking at me.

"It's such a different kind of rush, knowing they all came out to see me."

"They loved you," I tell her and hold her tighter.

It all happens too fast, and I miss the movement, but in the blink of an eye, her soft lips are on mine. The kiss is a shock to my system. It's unlike anything I've ever felt before, and I hope to experience many more. As her lips dance across mine, I move my hand into her hair and cup the back of her head, so I can deepen the kiss.

The moment she melts into me, her soft moan floats out. I take advantage by sneaking into her mouth with my tongue and stroking hers. When her body, which is pressed close to me, shivers, my dick wants inside her. My cock is already hard as nails, and when her hands tangle in my hair, I'm wanting to take her and keep going. There's no way to hide how hard I am either. There isn't an inch of space between us, and every time she moves, she brushes against my cock. She moans again, and I have enough presence of mind to remember where we are, and how exposed we are. I don't want anyone but me to hear those sounds, and I sure as hell don't want to get carried away any more than we already are here in the open.

Slowly, I pull back and rest my forehead on hers. We both catch our breath, as I run my hand through her hair because I can't seem to stop touching her.

"Ready to go check out the rides?" I ask, needing to put a bit of space between us before I find a room where we can continue that kiss.

"Let's do it." She flashes me a huge smile and pulls me into the crowd.

Chapter 9

Savannah

The show yesterday raised over ten thousand dollars for the charity alone. That's not including the donations collected and the money the rest of the carnival made.

I'm so excited to have been able to help. It's so much more fulfilling than killing myself on tour and not seeing a dime until it's over. Not that I have a need to spend it on anything. I was able to prepay my bills for the length of the tour since we didn't have time to go out and do anything.

I guess that's why I'm liking this break more than I thought I would. Less than two weeks ago, I thought it was the end of the world, and possibly, the end of my career. Now, I find it freeing, as I'm able to do things, like the show at the carnival yesterday and participate in the town's Secret Santa today.

Ford is coming over, and the four of us are going to get our names. Lilly and Mike have been talking about it all year. This is a new event. Apparently, the church ladies saw some Christmas movie about a town Secret Santa that led to two people falling in love and decided they just had to do an event like that in Rock Springs.

But this is Texas, so they put their own twist on it. You have to do something nice for the person. This way, those that don't have the money to spare don't have to spend money, just their time. They promised to give a list of things the person needs, along with the name.

It was fun to fill mine out. Mike, Lilly, and I sat down the other night, and they, of course, had on their list a bunch of work around the ranch and with the horses. My list was a little different. One thing I put down was research to find new charities to help, ones like Abby and Greg's that really need the assistance. Another couple of list items for me were helping me deliver Christmas cookies around town, and in the off chance, a lawyer gets my name, help with my contract.

That last one is a long shot. But hey, a girl can dream. So now, I'm in Mike's truck and heading with Lilly and Mike to the church to see who we got.

Just like I expected, the town is more crowded with people, who are not even bothering to hide their cameras. Apparently, Jason put a sign up on the bar that no cameras were allowed inside, and Jo followed suit with the diner. For the first time ever, she went as far as to pull the shades down in her windows.

I haven't voiced what it means to me that the town is trying to protect me, but I have a feeling Lilly already knows because she's keeping up with it all. Needing to take my mind off of it, I turn to Ford.

"What did you put on your list?" I ask him.

"Work around the ranch, redecorating the house, and help with my Christmas shopping."

I laugh, "Anything to get out of shopping."

"Not really. I know what I want to get everyone, but it does require a few runs into Dallas. If I can have someone do that for me, it will give me enough time to get stuff done on the ranch. Or if they don't want to shop, they can do some chores here, while I shop in Dallas. Either way, it's the same result."

"And hopefully, you can avoid the city." I tease him.

"That too, though I don't mind Dallas, because I know the city. It's the cities that I don't know that I'm not a fan of."

"I understand that more than you know," I say and look out of the window.

As we pull in at the church, everyone is excited to see who they're going to get. It's part of the fun, like opening a present on Christmas. A quick glance around shows there aren't any photographers here. I guess they don't expect me to show up at the church since I'm not known to go to one on tour.

"Okay, remember we get our names and no opening them until we get home," Lilly says, and we all agree.

We go in, and Mrs. Willow greets us.

"Alright, this is very simple. Let's try not to mess this up!" She levels us with a glare that says people have already messed it up.

"You are going to find your name on one of the Christmas trees. Men are on the side with the white trees, and the ladies are on this side with the green trees. On top of the tree, there are a few letters. It goes by the first letter of your first name. So, Lilly finds the green tree with the Letter L and then looks for the envelope with her name on it. There are signs everywhere that explain this. Don't screw this up." Then, she shakes a finger at us, and we all laugh.

"I feel like there's a story behind your speech, Mrs. Willow."

"Sweetheart, you have no idea. With the kids these days, the whole world is in trouble." She goes off on a tangent, as she starts organizing papers on the table, where she's sitting.

We split up and go find our trees. It really is pretty easy to find my envelope, which is at the back of the tree. I meet Lilly and the guys by the front door, and Mrs. Willow verifies we have gotten the correct envelope before we go back out to Mike's truck.

On the way home, all I want to do is open my envelope.

"Whose idea was it anyway to wait, until we got home to open these? We should have done it in the truck." I say, annoyed we have to wait a whole fifteen more minutes until we get back to the ranch.

"I second that," Mike grumbles, making us all laugh.

"We will be home in a few minutes. It's not that bad." Lilly laughs and rubs his arm. Watching Mike visibly relax under her touch, makes me ache to find what they have. I want it more than anything; more than I want to go back on the tour, even though I won't admit that out loud to anyone.

"So maybe, we should take a day and go up to Dallas to do a bit of shopping, and we can figure out what to do for the people we get? Maybe, tomorrow?" Lilly suggests.

I already know Ford won't go. He's going to wait to see if he can get his Secret Santa to do the shopping, and he's already mentioned he has too much to do. I, on the other hand, have an almost completely free schedule.

"I'd be up for a shopping trip, but you know that," I smile.

"Where you go, I go," Mike says once again, making me ache for the love they have.

Lilly looks at Ford.

"Come on! We'll make a day out of it," Lilly says.

Ford looks over at me, and I smile. I want him to come, and hope he'll say yes.

"Well, I guess I can't let Savannah be the third wheel to you two, because I know what that's like."

Lilly cheers, as we pull into her driveway. I smile over at Ford, and his smile matches mine. He's more excited to go than he's letting on.

We all head inside and sit in the living room. Lilly makes a big deal out of each of us, opening our envelopes one at a time. She lets Mike go first, joking about how impatient he is, only it's not really a joke, and we all know patience isn't his strong suit.

"Alright, I got Brice." He says and looks at Ford.

"I can tell you without even looking at his list. He needs help with organizing his office more than anything. Joy, his receptionist, is out of town visiting family like she does every year. Normally, his mom stops in to help, and he gets by, but she had surgery and isn't able to this year."

"I can help you with that. We can make a day out of it," Lilly says.

"Okay, easy enough." Mike sets his card down.

"How did you know that?" I ask Ford.

"Brice and I grew up together, and next to Mike, he's one of my best friends." Ford shrugs like it's no big deal.

To me, people knowing you and knowing what you need help with is a big deal. Do they know how special a community like this is? How rare it is? I hope so.

"Lilly, you go next," I say, trying to shake the thoughts from my head.

"Oh! I got Abby!" She smiles big.

"What's on her list?" Mike asks, leaning over to read the paper.

"Two things. Helping her study and helping wrap up The Winter Carnival. That's great, and we can do both," she says.

"Yep, I can help out with the carnival, and you can help her study," Mike says.

There they go again. No matter that this is supposed to be a person-to-person thing, they are still a team. It's almost too much.

"You go next, Savannah," Ford says, pulling me from my thoughts once again.

I open my envelope.

"I got Anna Mae. She needs help setting up and organizing the nursery. Oh, that's going to be so much fun!" I say, suddenly very excited. I already have ideas running through my head.

So, they have a gift to open under the tree, I can pick up something small and wrap it.

"Okay, Ford. You're up." Everyone turns to look at him. "I got Mac. Looks like he needs some assistance around the ranch and help to plan a surprise for his family on Christmas day."

"What kind of surprise?" I ask.

"It doesn't say, so I guess I'll have to go talk to him and find out."

"Oh, this is so exciting!" Lilly says, almost bouncing out of her seat.

I have to admit it's fun, but now, I wonder who got me.

Chapter 10

Ford

"Candy Cane Donuts, really?" Savannah asks as we pull into the bakery.

"Yes, and you are going to fall in love with them," Lilly says, as we get out of the car.

Today, we are in Dallas doing some Christmas shopping, and while I really had no plans to come into the city, I wasn't going to miss spending some time with Savannah.

We have spent the day running around and shopping downtown. When Savannah dragged us into a baby store to get some things for Anna Mae and Royce, we all groaned.

So far, I was able to knock Brice and my parents off my shopping list, and then we had lunch and walked it off, and now, we're at the bakery. It's a crime to go into Dallas this time of year and not come stop at the bakery.

When I hold the door open for Savannah, Mike then takes it from me to hold it open for Lilly. I have noticed today we work well taking care of the girls, and I hope that's a good sign.

After her show, we had that kiss, but there hasn't been another one. Though, she hasn't been shy about letting me hold her hand today. We also haven't really had a moment alone to talk about it, but I want to find a way to have some alone time with her.

If nothing else, just to see where her head is, but at best, because I'd love another kiss.

"Wow, this place doesn't mess around on the Christmas decorations," Savannah says in wonder, as she steps into the bakery.

"No, they don't," I say, as I place a hand on her lower back and guide her to the line, as she takes the store in.

The bakery is spotless with modern decor. Lots of white, well, everything is white. For Christmas, they have brought in a lot of red and silver decorations. From the ceiling hanging at all different lengths, there are large red and silver balls. They are designed to look like Christmas tree decorations, but they are the size of a beach ball.

The counters, cabinets, floors, and tables are all white, and they have done a great job bringing in the red décor, making it look magical. There's a small sitting area off to the side, and we're fortunate to find an open table.

"Why don't you girls grab that table, and we will get a snack. When we get ready to leave, we can grab some goodies to take home," I tell them, and Mike nods in agreement.

The girls link arms and stroll over to the table. I know Savannah has been worried about being spotted today and ruining the fun, but the few times she was stopped, it seems like Mike and Lilly were just as excited for her, as I have been.

Whenever she can, Savannah has been wearing a baseball hat with her hair tucked up under it and sunglasses. Even casual and without makeup, she still looks stunningly beautiful.

Mike and I get into line, and he turns to me just as expected.

"So, what's going on with the two of you?" He nods towards the table where the girls are.

"I'm not sure. We had a great time at the carnival, but we haven't been able to have any time alone since." I smirk at him because he already knows that.

"So, nothing's happened?" He asks.

"We kissed," I say because I'm guessing he already knows that. Savannah probably told Lilly, and I know Lilly would have told Mike.

"And?" He asks.

Thinking about that kiss again, I can't stop smiling.

"It was a life changing kiss." Mike smiles, and I know he's happy for me.

"You know you need to be careful though, right? I want you both happy, but she will be out of town the first chance she gets. She has dreams that don't include Rock Springs."

"I know." I sigh and shove my hands into my pockets. "But I can't deny what I'm feeling for her. I have to believe, if it's meant to be, it will work out. I get that more than likely I will end up with my heart broken, but that's a chance I'm willing to take."

"You're a brave man. I had to take that risk with Lilly, too. She was a truck driver and always on the road. But I got lucky, and a blizzard trapped her here and gave her time to figure out what she wanted."

"I doubt I will get that lucky, but I damn sure plan on trying," I tell him, as I watch the girls leaning over Lilly's phone and giggling.

When it's our turn, we get donuts, peppermint hot chocolate, and some peppermint bark, before sitting down at the table.

Putting everything down, I sit next to Savannah and pull her chair closer to mine. I just want her near me, and she doesn't seem to mind, because she leans against me.

"Are these the ones they kept talking about last year?" Savannah asks Lilly.

"Yeah, there's also candy cane fudge that they now carry all year, but I just call it peppermint fudge. Ella was thrilled, because she craved it all summer, and the guys on the ranch made a few special trips into Dallas just for her," Lilly says.

Savannah takes the first sip of her hot chocolate and smiles. "This is good." Then, she takes a bite of the donut.

"It's official. I will be in Dallas every Christmas now, and I'm hooked."

Lilly smiles, and I'm sure she's excited to have family near, but all I can think is that I need her more than just Christmas and have to find a way to make that happen.

My head tries to go to war with my heart, saying it's just one kiss. It's too early to be making plans like this. My heart is saying that one kiss told us everything we need to know, so yes, we can.

Before I know it, we're done and placing our order to take home. I get a box of donuts for the ranch hands, and a box for the main house because I know Brice will be over, and that man can eat half a dozen in one sitting. Savannah, Mike, and Lilly get a few boxes each with plans to take them to Blaze and Riley's at the ranch, and some for their ranch hands, too.

No sooner are we out of the Dallas city limits does Savannah's phone ring.

"Sorry, it's a Nashville number. I should take this." Everyone quietens down, as she answers the phone.

Trying to give her as much privacy as possible, while sharing a back seat with her, I pull out my phone and start going through the ranch emails and checking in with my senior ranch hand. He tells me everything is going smoothly and better me than him in the city today.

Not many important emails, but lots of stuff I just trash, so when I'm able to sit down again, the important stuff is ready to go.

"Are you serious?" Savannah says, catching my attention.

I look over at her, and it seems to be a good thing, because her eyes are wide, and she's smiling.

"Of course, I can be there." She pauses again. "Yes, I know where that is." Another pause. "Yes, you can text it to this number."

She continues to listen, nodding her head, like whoever is on the other line can see her.

"Can I ask who told you about this?" She asks.

A moment later, she bursts out laughing and shakes her head.

"Thank you so much. I'll see you in just a few days," she says.

My heart sinks. A Nashville number, and she'll see them in a few days, means she's leaving. I thought I had more time, but like Mike said, she's out of here the first chance she gets.

Before Savannah can hang up the phone, Lilly is turning around from the front passenger seat to face her.

"So, who was it?" She's feeding off of Savannah's excitement.

"So, you know the band Highway 55, right?"

"Oh, my yes. Landon is so damn hot. Too bad he recently got married," Lilly says.

"Hey, and you are married!" Mike playfully swats Lilly's leg.

"Of course, I meant if I hadn't met you, dear," Lilly says in a way you know she doesn't truly mean it, but we all laugh, anyway.

"Well, both guys are now married, and they wanted to settle down, so they started their own record label," Savannah says.

"I heard about that." Lilly interrupts. "It was big news, because they were supposedly in the height of their career, and they just had the most popular song of their career, *'She's Still the One.'*"

"Exactly. Well, that was Dallas, and he wants me to come in to talk about my current contract and possibly working together. He says he's been following what happened in the news, and he knows how the press is. They kept calling him playboy long after he had changed by doing exactly what they did to me."

"But don't you have over a year left on your contract?" Lilly asks.

"Yes, but Dallas seems to think my manager is in violation, because of something that's standard in the contracts from my label. He asked me to meet with him, so I need to leave tomorrow."

Just like that, barely any notice, and she's gone. I look out of the window, trying to hide my disappointment. This could be huge for her career, and I really am happy for her.

Her hand on my arm causes me to turn back to her.

"It's just for a few days, and if you're able to get away from the ranch, I'd really like you to join me. I think you'll love Nashville at Christmas," she says.

That's a hook I didn't expect. It gives me hope that maybe she felt the same way about the kiss that I did.

"I don't think it's such a good idea," I say, but my mind starts whirling at the ways I can make it happen. This is the best time of the year to getaway.

"Even though I get it, I really don't want to go alone." The vulnerability in her voice seals the deal.

"I might be able to make it happen. How long will we be gone?"

A huge smile takes over her face, and I know Lilly and Mike are both watching us.

"If possible, I'd like two days in Nashville, one for the meeting, and one to show you around, and then a day traveling there and back."

"I can do that." I nod, knowing my ranch hands would kick my ass if I turned this down. Heck, my parents, too.

"Thank you!" She leans over and kisses my cheek. "I'll book our flights, as soon as we get home."

"I can get my own flight." I start to tell her.

"Nope. I asked you to come, so I'll cover the flight. Plus, the record label is putting us up at The Gaylord Hotel right next to The Grand Ole Opry."

"Okay." I agree, knowing I can cover meals and everything else, while we're there.

"So, get this! I asked him how he heard about everything, and do you know what he said?"

"What?" I ask.

"He was told to tell me my Secret Santa contacted him. Who in Rock Springs has those kinds of connections?"

Lilly and Mike look at each other at the same time, and then say, "Sage."

I chuckle because it's true. That girl traveled for a while after school and made so many connections it still blows my mind. Then, she came back to Rock Springs and helped expand her family's ranch.

"This was my crazy goal to find someone to go over my contract." She widens her eyes, and her voice shakes in awe.

"Why? I thought you loved being on tour? I know this has been a little setback and all." Lilly asks, reading my mind.

"I was too scared to voice it, but the tour isn't really all I want to do with the rest of my life. But it's all my manager wants me to do, because it makes him money," she says.

"It's always good to keep your options open. Even if you were crazy happy with your record label and manager, I'd have said to take the meeting," I tell her.

"That's what Mom would have said too, and you know it," Lilly adds.

"You're right. Now, try not to get my hopes up, before the meeting."

All I can think is now it's time for me not to get my hopes up, and that she can find a way to stay.

Chapter 11
Savannah

I love Nashville at Christmas and can't wait to show it to Ford. As we step into the airport, the Christmas decor is everywhere, and Christmas music is on the speakers overhead.

Pulling my hat down a little more, hoping I'm not recognized, I take Ford's hand.

We had a talk yesterday, and I offered to let him back out because if I'm recognized, his face would be all over the tabloids. Who knows what they would say about it. Though Ford didn't seem to care, and he was more worried if I'd be okay with it.

As we get to the part of the airport where families are greeting loved ones, Ford pulls on my hand.

"Is that for you?" He points to a driver holding a sign that says Savannah with H55 in the corner.

I walk up and smile at the older man. "Dallas send you?"

"Yes, ma'am. Let me take your bags; right this way."

The bulky man beside him starts walking with us, and when I look over, he nods.

"I'm Mason. I work security for Landon and Dallas, and they sent me to make sure there are no issues."

He doesn't have to finish the sentence. He means any paparazzi who try to get too close, or if any attention is drawn to me.

"Please, tell them I appreciate it," I tell him, as we step outside, and the cool air hits me.

Dennis got a great parking spot, and we get in the back of a large SUV, while he loads our bags.

Taking off my hat and glasses, I look over at Ford. He is taking it all in, but he's relaxed and almost fits right in, despite how out of his element I know he feels.

I snuggle up to him in the backseat, as the driver gets in, and we make our way out of the airport.

"I didn't expect a car, as I was going to rent one," I say to them.

The driver smiles.

"If Landon and Dallas are trying to sign you to the label, they'll pull out all the stops. They're that good at what they do."

When we pull up to the hotel, the driver gets out and checks us in, and then joins us to give us our room's info.

"Let me get your bags," he offers.

"It's okay. We got them. Thanks for all of this."
I tell him.

"I'm to walk you to your room," Mason says,
and then follows us into the hotel.

The Gaylord is known for its massive atrium
that has plants, rivers, and waterfalls. This is the
main hub of the hotels. There are restaurants
and bars all here set to enjoy the view. Heck,
they even offer a boat ride on the river.

Decorated for Christmas, there are Christmas
lights and festive decor everywhere, and we
take time out to enjoy it on the way to our room.

No sooner than we get into our room than
Dallas calls.

"How was your flight?" He asks.

"It was great, thanks to you. Pulling out all the
stops for me, aren't you?"

"Well," Dallas says. "It's no secret I know how
the press can be, and I think you have had
enough of them for the time being."

"That's the truth."

"Well, relax and go grab dinner. There's some
great food there at the hotel. I'll see you tomorrow."

"See you then."

• • • • ● • ● • • •

"Hello, I have a meeting with Landon and Dallas," I say to the woman at the front desk.

"Savannah! Of course. I'm Deanna. If you need anything, just shout. I'll let them know you're here."

She's bubbly and full of energy. Without a doubt, she's a great face for the label.

I barely get a chance to sit down, when a woman who looks familiar, but I can't place steps into the room.

"Hey, I'm Austin, Dallas's wife. I wasn't supposed to be here today, but I came in to do some work on their website and convinced him that I could be useful talking to you." She winks at me, as she shakes my hand.

"I bet it didn't take much convincing," Deanna giggles.

"Oh, you know it. You're coming by tonight for book club, right?" Austin says with a big smile.

"Wouldn't miss it, except for maybe that new singer the guys just signed. Whew, he's a hottie." She says, fanning herself.

I love they are friends, and that says a lot about the mood here. One I really like versus the cold and almost sterile environment at my current label.

"Come on, let's head back," Austin says to me, as I follow her down the hallway she just came from.

Entering the room, it reminds me more of a living room than a meeting room. Plush leather couches and chairs form a long rectangle with a row of coffee tables down the center.

There's a large mounted flat screen TV in one corner, a table of drinks in another, and large floor to ceiling windows with a great view onto Music Row.

"Savannah!" Two men stand up and greet me.

Austin introduces us, "This is my husband, Dallas, and my brother, Landon. You know them as the band Highway 55."

Landon shakes my hand first, and I can see the resemblance. Austin has the same dark brown hair and the same gray eyes.

"We're so glad you made the trip. We have been watching your videos and are excited to talk to you." Landon says, sitting down in one of the chairs.

"Though we're sorry you're dealing with the media backlash right now, but we have a few ideas," Dallas adds, before sitting on the couch next to Landon's chair.

When Austin goes to sit next to him, he pulls her sideways onto his lap.

"Dallas! This isn't very professional." Austin scolds him, but settles more into him, anyway.

"We aren't very professional here, baby girl," Dallas says, chuckling while wrapping his arms around her. Even Landon has a smirk on his face, and I can only imagine what things were like when they started dating.

Almost like she can read my mind, Austin turns to me.

"The press liked playboy Dallas. Honestly, they still do. He tried to change, but they would write whatever story they wanted. To this day, they still try to start rumors and split us up. Even though they don't like the idea of a re-formed playboy, the fans do."

I think of Ford, who is back at the hotel, saying he was going to talk with his parents and sister and go over emails, while he waited for me. How will he do with all the press? Will he ignore the rumors and trust me?

"Yes," I say in agreement. "It seems like they will do anything for sales. Hell, I was friends with the guy's wife and liked her better than him, but here we are." I sigh, feeling like I keep repeating myself, trying to change people's minds.

"So, you're in Texas right now?" Landon asks.

"Yeah, my sister and her husband live there in a tiny town. They remind me a lot of you two." I smile over at Dallas and Austin. "My parents are on vacation, but they will be joining us for Christmas at my sister's place."

"That's where you did the charity concert?" Dallas asks.

"Yeah, the church puts on a winter carnival every year, and the proceeds go to help people around town. The pastor just got married recently, and his wife is studying to be a midwife. It was her idea to start a charity to help new parents with some things they might need for the baby. All the money for the concert went straight to that fund."

"You didn't worry that it would give away where you were hiding to the press?" Landon asks.

"Yes, but the town voted, and they agreed they would deal with whatever came. Rock Springs is the kind of small-town where the gossip flows freely, but they don't take kindly to outsiders. And because Lilly is so well loved, they accepted me, too." I say.

"It's just like those books you're always reading." Dallas kisses Austin's cheek, and they both smile.

"It's the kind of place I wish I could live, but as you know, you have to be here or Los Angles, if you want a music career."

"Very true," Landon says.

"Well, we looked over the contract you sent over and had our lawyer look it over, too. Just like we thought, it's a standard contract from the label. But they have been doing things for so long, that they haven't really updated things. Plus, I'm sorry, but your manager is cocky. He seems to think you need him more than he needs you because you aren't the tour headliner," Dallas says.

"Okay?" I ask, still not sure where things are going.

"In short, they are in breach of contract. You didn't break any rules on the tour, and you can't help how you're photographed. There's no reason to cancel tour dates for you. In addition, there are a few other things the contract states that I don't see your manager doing either," Landon says.

I'm not sure what to say, or where they are going with this, and thankfully, Austin steps in.

"Geeze, guys. You are worse than the lawyers sometimes. To summarize everything, they can get you out of your contract with the label and your manager, and even sue for loss of royalties. It will free you up to go to any label of your choice, but now, they will give you their pitch on why we'd like you to join us." Austin says, smiling big.

"She never did beat around the bush." Landon chuckles. "It was such a pain growing up when I was trying to butter up Mom and Dad for something."

Austin just shrugs, but you can see the love and pride between them. It's a lot like the relationship Lilly and I have.

"She's right. We will help you out of this contract, even if you don't sign with us," Dallas says.

"Why?"

"A favor to a friend," Dallas smirks.

"I was meaning to ask how you guys knew
Sage," I smirk back.

The guys look at each other then back at me.

"We don't personally. Sage is friends with
Deanna's sister, and when Deanna heard about
you, she mentioned it to us. Then, Sage mentioned the contract and here we are."

I shake my head because Sage and I aren't that
close, but I know how much family means to
her. Since Riley is Sage's sister-in-law, and Lilly
not only saved Riley's life, but they are now best
friends and part of the family. She sees me as a
family just because I'm Lilly's sister.

That kind of unconditional support is something I'm still trying to get used to. For so long,
I trusted no one, but my family, but things are
so different in Rock Springs, so it's easy to let
my guard down.

"Ready to hear our pitch?" Landon asks.

Thankful for the change in the topic, I nod.

"Okay, so we did our homework and see that
you are big on helping out charities," Landon
says.

"Not just any charities, but smaller ones that
don't get a lot of publicity," Austin adds.

"That's right. So, we'd like to give you some options for more of that. We have been working with some music-related charities ourselves. One of our programs is getting music into schools and helping with after-school music programs. We are also partnering with Oak-side Rehabilitation Center down in Georgia. They work with wounded military veterans, and they're starting up music therapy."

"That's exactly the kind of thing I love helping with. I, um, also help with domestic abuse charities. My sister saved her best friend from a situation like that, and while I don't talk about it much, I was in a bad relationship, before I started singing, though I was very lucky. Many others aren't," I admit.

Usually, I don't open up so soon after meeting people, but maybe, it's this atmosphere, where it feels more like friends hanging out.

Thankfully, they don't pry, but take it in stride.

"We'd like to work with you on whatever charities you choose. Ideally, we'd like to see you pick one to partner with, and then become the face of it. Of course, you can work with others, but putting yourself as the face of a charity, will be the main goal," Landon says.

Dallas interjects, "Our tours are much more relaxed as well. You get time to enjoy the city and sightseeing. When fans think they can run into you at their favorite coffee shop or store, they see you as more approachable and connect better."

"I was on tour with them, before Dallas and I started dating," Austin adds. "And one of the stops was Asheville, North Carolina. The day before the concert we were able to visit The Biltmore Estate. I think that was the day that pushed our relationship into motion."

"I agree," Dallas says softly more for Austin than us.

Landon pulls out a contract and spends the next thirty minutes going over it and pointing out several clauses to pay attention to, such as no drug use. Neither me nor anyone working with me.

I heard they started that when they were on tour, and it's taking off around the music industry here in Nashville. Their own label has put it in all their contracts now, too. Some artists are making it mandatory in their contracts at other labels.

My current label snickers at the idea and wouldn't even entertain it when I brought it up for my contract renewal.

Then, they go over their tour schedules and talk about how, while tours are important, they now have some other great ways to promote the music. Ways that allow their artists to be home more than on the road.

The more I talk to them, the more I see a different life ahead of me, and the more I want it. One that isn't so controlled, and a tour that I can actually enjoy the craft again.

"When do I need to get back to you guys on this?" I ask as we finish up.

"We don't want to hear from you, before the first of the year," Austin says, shocking me a bit. I was thinking I'd have forty-eight hours at most.

"You'll see we do things differently here. It's the holidays, and while it's not right kicking you off the tour, it does allow you to be with family. So, spend time with your family, take some downtime, think it over, and reflect on how you want your career to look like. This contract isn't set in stone. Think of it as a negotiation," Landon says.

"Come back to see us with some ideas or requests, but not before the first of the year. We're giving the office and our staff the time between Christmas and the New Year off, and we're taking our wives on vacation," Dallas says.

"Thank you again for everything," I tell them.

I have a lot to think about, but right now, all I can think about is getting back to the hotel and telling Ford everything.

Chapter 12

Ford

Just as I send an email off to my ranch manager, Savannah comes busting through the hotel room door.

"How was your meeting?" I ask.

"Better than I hoped." Then, she flops down on the bed and starts telling me about the meeting, the contract, and their offer.

Her eyes light up, as she talks about their offer to join them and work with her own charities. Then, she launches into speaking about the charities they are already helping out, and how she looked them up on the way back here.

I love the light in her eyes, and the energy she has talking about this. But I know this is where her heart is, and I push away the part of my brain yelling that to have it, she needs to be here in Nashville. Though I don't want to ruin this trip with her, instead I want it as a memory to soak up and look back on.

"I don't even know how to repay Sage for this. This is huge. I feel like I owe her my firstborn child now."

Chuckling, I say, "I doubt she expects that."

Sage is the kindest person I know, though, she has a hard exterior and cusses as much as any cowboy. In her defense, she had to grow up fast, because her birth parents weren't the nicest people. But she got lucky being adopted into Blaze's family, and she will do something for someone she barely knows, and then expect nothing for it in return. She's always been that way, too.

While she and Brice dated for a hot second, it wasn't long, before Colt stepped in and claimed her. But Brice has nothing bad to say about her, which is a miracle because he always finds something about every girl he's dated.

"Well," Savannah says. "I need to do something. Let's get out there and enjoy the day in Nashville because we have dinner plans with Dallas and Austin tonight."

"More contract talk?" I ask.

I don't mind the contract talks, and I could sit and watch her talk business all day, if she lights up the way she did, when she was talking about it earlier.

"Nope, this is a couple's dinner, and they want to offer support about the press and meet you," she shrugs.

"Can't wait to meet them. Though, don't get mad, because I plan to ask them for something signed for my sister for Christmas."

To get her something, while I'm here, is a no brainier. She loves country music, and especially Highway 55, so I'll rock Christmas this year. Though, I'll probably never be able to top it again in my life.

"I'll try to pretend not to be embarrassed by you. Now, on to pay tribute to one of the greatest music men ever to walk the earth." She takes my hand.

"Elvis? I thought he was in Memphis." I say, honestly confused.

"Bite your damn tongue! I was talking about Johnny Cash!"

The driver Dallas and Landon gave us for our time here takes us downtown and drops us off in front of the brick building that holds the museum. We spend the next hour walking through the museum that takes you chronologically through the history of Johnny Cash.

There's even a small theater with about twenty-five chairs that's playing clips from the different TV shows that Johnny Cash was in. *Dr. Quinn Medicine Woman* is playing, when we visit.

As we get further into the museum, there are some photos with him and Elvis, and I don't miss the glare Savannah gives me, and I can't help but smirk. Riling her up is kind of fun, and I like keeping her on her toes.

When stepping back out onto the sidewalk in the cool fresh air, Savannah pulls out her phone.

"Where to next?" I ask because I'm sure she has the whole day planned.

"A light lunch at the fried chicken food truck. It's one of my favorites, and I saw it's going to be only two blocks away. Let's go." She grabs my hand and starts pulling me back towards the main row with all the country bars on it.

Obviously, she knows this town and is at home here. The country bars even now have music floating out to the street mixed with the smell of stale beer and all things fried bar food.

The neon lights overhead aren't on in the bright light of day, but I can imagine this street lit up at night with all the colors going. It's such a night and day difference than grabbing a drink at WJ's back in Rock Springs.

Sure enough, two blocks ups on the corner is a food truck with a line, but it seems to be moving pretty fast.

"Eat light. Dallas and Austin sound like they are planning a feast." She warns as we get in line.

The girls, who get in line behind us recognize her and ask for her autograph and a photo. We got stopped a few times in the Johnny

Cash Museum as well, and she handled it with grace. When asked, she was always gracious and smiled, while signing autographs and posing for pictures.

It's a lot like going out in Rock Springs, I guess. You can't go out anywhere without being stopped by someone, who wants to talk to you about something. The only difference there is you know the people, and they know you. But I'm thinking I prefer that to strangers walking up to us on the sidewalk.

"You're good with them," I say when she joins me back in line.

"I do this for the music, yes. But there would be no music without the fans, so I always make time for them. I'm not that popular, so it's not a mob scene, like when the band would go out."

Stepping up, we place our order for some fried chicken sliders, but when Savannah tries to pull out her wallet, I grab her hand.

"I said I'm paying." I remind her, and she gives in, but I know she will try again. Though she can try all she wants, I'm sticking to my guns on this. I'm not here for a free ride, and I can take care of her and plan to if she will only let me.

As we eat, we walk back slowly towards the museum. While I prefer to sit down and eat, just about everyone on the street has food, or drinks, or shopping bags in their hands, so we fit right in.

We spend the rest of the afternoon seeing the sights, and she has the driver take me for a drive down music row. It's a bonus that the driver is able to give us some juicy details on the labels. Finally, we stop at some local shops and get gifts for those back home.

Before I know it, it's time to head to Dallas and Austin's for dinner. They live just outside the city limits where things are much more spread out than in the city and much more my pace.

Their home is one of those old southern homes that you know they have restored and given some love, too.

Before we even get to the front door, a man and a woman greet us.

The woman hugs Savannah, asking, "Did you have fun out on the town?" Then, her eyes find me. "This must be Ford."

Savannah smiles and says to me, "This is Austin, Dallas's wife. Dallas and Austin's brother Landon are better known as the band Highway 55." Taking my hand, she adds, "This is Ford." I notice the lack of a title, and Austin smirks like it doesn't escape her either. Though in Savannah's place, I'm not sure what I'd call us either. Maybe, I need to make my intentions clearer, when we get back to the room.

We spend a few hours talking and eating. They share stories from out on the road and do very well to include me in the conversation. Austin is fascinated by the workings of the ranch, and I find myself telling her and her husband to come out and visit sometime, and that I'd be happy to put them to work.

The food is delicious, and Austin admits she and her brother share a chef to help make sure they eat with how busy their lives have been, starting the label.

It turns out that Savannah is the one to ask for a signed photo for my sister, which Dallas is happy to do. He even takes a photo with me to prove to her I actually met him.

Before I know it, we're heading out again.

"I feel like you just got here," Austin says, hugging Savannah goodbye.

"I know, but I want to take him through the drive-through Christmas lights, and we have an early tour of The Grand Ole Opry tomorrow," she says.

"Okay well, if you need anything, you let us know, even if it's just a place to eat," Dallas says, as we get in the car.

The car is different than the SUV we were picked up in. This one has more space and a privacy window.

"I figured with the long drive you'd like a little more room." The chauffeur says with a smile, before closing the door. It's a bit of a drive back into town, but by the time we get there, it's dark and perfect for viewing the lights.

The lights are synced to a Christmas station on the radio, and upbeat Christmas music fills the air.

"This is incredible," I say, taking it all in.

"It is, and I wanted to make sure you saw it. It's one of my favorite things about Christmas here."

As she turns to look at the lights, she takes my hand, but I don't like her on the other side of the car. With a quick movement, I unbuckle her and wrap my arm around her waist, pulling her to my side.

She lets out the most adorable little squeak, before snuggling into my side. When the first song comes to an end, she looks up at me and smiles. I lean down and place a soft kiss on her lips, before pulling away much sooner than I'd like.

The smile is still there on her face a moment later, while we both go to watch the light show, going on just outside the windows. As the lights twinkle and dance, the car floods with bright colors.

She places her hand on my leg just above my knee, and I squeeze her hip. We keep playing this game of how close we can get. How much can we drive each other crazy, and who will break first.

By the time we finish with the light show, we're both breathing hard and an inch away from where we really want each other. When the door opens once back at the hotel, the cool air does nothing to help either of us cool down.

We race back to our room, and before the door even closes, I have her pinned to the door, and my lips back on hers.

This is no gentle lovemaking session. We are both on edge from the car ride, and she's ripping my shirt off, before removing hers. I grab a condom from my wallet before clothes go flying, and she's pushing me towards the bed. By the time I'm sitting on the bed, we're both completely naked.

Sitting there on the edge, I stare up at the sexy as hell woman in front of me. Tan skin, long legs, and a dancer's body from all her time on stage.

"You are the most beautiful person I've ever seen," I say because all other words escape me.

She doesn't say anything, just takes the condom from me and sinks to her knees between my legs. She kisses the tip of my cock, as she rips open the condom wrapper, and then slides it on.

Pulling her back up, she straddles me, as I sit on the edge of the bed. She leans down, and her lips meet mine, as I tug her to me. When she starts sliding against my cock, it feels so damn good. She's hot and wet, and I'm not even inside her yet.

I knead her soft ass cheeks and pull her closer without breaking our kiss.

"Don't tease me, Ford." She whispers against my lips.

"Wouldn't dream of it." I grip her hips, line the tip of my cock to her pussy, and slowly slide her down. We both moan as I stretch her with each inch of me, but she takes me right to the hilt. Pausing, I take a minute to breathe.

"Don't move." I grit out. "You're warm, wet, and are already pulsing around me. It's too much."

She's breathing hard, and her diamond hard nipples are brushing against my chest with each breath. When a shiver runs through her whole body, I'm done. There would be no holding back if I tried.

Gripping her hips, I slowly move her against me. After only a few thrusts, she sits up straight and takes control, sinking further on to me each time, while picking up the pace.

When she begins moving faster, I strum her clit, and she throws her head back. With her glossy brown hair, tumbling down her back, she's gorgeous. Then, her moans get louder, and her grip on my shoulders tightens. Watching her let go like this with me, is something I won't ever forget. I know how much trust that takes, especially from her.

I try to memorize every detail. The flush on her cheeks, how her lips part, the marks on her breast from my chest hair rubbing against them, but mostly, I memorize the feel of her pussy starting to clamp down on me.

When I'm a second from not being able to hold off anymore, she screams out her orgasm, as her entire body tenses. I let go and come harder than I have in my life.

She wraps herself around me, not wanting to let go or to let me move. I have no intention of going anywhere. If I could, I'd sleep like this. Certainly, I don't want to pull out of her, but I need to get both of us cleaned up. When I roll us over and lay her on the bed, the satisfied lazy smile on her face says it all. Kissing the top of her head, I hurry and get cleaned up.

Nothing could keep me from that bed with her tonight. Nothing.

Chapter 13

Savannah

I slowly wake up in the most comfortable bed I've ever been in. I'm cozy and happy, but that fades the moment I try to turn over, and a strong arm pulls me closer to the warm body next to me.

Looking over, Ford is next to me, and last night comes flooding back to me. The touches, the kisses, and the orgasms. I now understand why the phrase *'Ride a Cowboy'* is so popular. Everyone needs to do it at least once in their life.

Attempting again to move and get out of bed, the arm tightens around me once more. "Stop trying to sneak out of bed." He mumbles without even opening his eyes.

"I'm not trying to sneak out. I have to pee." I lean over and kiss his forehead, but he pulls me in for a real kiss. One that says good morning in a devilish way.

Lazily, his hands run down the side of my body to my hips and back up, driving me crazy.

"We don't have time for that, because we have a tour this morning." I remind him, and he groans and turns over, allowing me to get up. I freshen up, before walking back out of the bathroom naked, and his eyes heat, when he sees me.

"You tell me we can't do this, and then have the nerve to walk out here looking like that?" He growls, and faster than this man should be able to, he pulls me onto the bed and is over me, resting between my thighs.

"You are just going to have to be late," he states, as he slides into me nice and slow.

We both groan at the pleasure, and I have a brief thought that I need to stop for a moment. But then, he tilts his hips and kisses me on the lips, and I have no idea why we should stop. The only thoughts in my mind are how perfectly he's stretching me, and how I want more. Much more.

Another shift of his hips and pleasure rolls through me so fast, that it's like a tidal wave. I start coming on his cock, the scream lodged in my throat. How can this man play my body so well, after just one night?

The moment I feel his hot release in me, it sets off another orgasm, and I swear I blackout, because the next thing I know, he's kissing my neck ever so lightly and tenderly. He's still inside of me and on top of me, but he's holding his weight up enough to not crush me.

"Now, we can get ready." He says, pulling out, and as he starts to get up, he freezes.

"What's wrong?" I ask, sitting up as well.

That's when I feel his warm release on my thigh.

"I forgot the condom." He stares at where his come is leaking out of me.

"I'm on the shot, so we're covered. And it's been a really long time, since I've been with anyone, and I've been tested since, too." I tell him.

His eyes shoot to me, and he growls. Yes, the caveman growls and is on top of me again.

"You have my come leaking out of you, and you're talking about other men?" He nips at my ear, and then I do something I haven't done during sex in as long as I can remember. I laugh.

Ford whispers in my ear, "I'm clean too, and it's been a really long time for me, too." Then, he kisses me again.

"But to be clear, if anything were to happen, I'm going to be there, and I will take care of you both. Do you understand me?"

I just nod, because my throat is so tight, and for a moment, I pray his seed takes root because the flash of a life I see with him tugs at my heart. When he kisses me again, I get a moment to put that wall in place, before we are up and getting ready.

Surprisingly, we make it to The Grand Ole Opry with two minutes to spare. The entire time, Ford never once let go of my hand, as we tour backstage of the dressing rooms.

The tours end with us on the stage, and something about being center stage at The Grand Ole Opry, even with all the seats empty, I freeze. Ford walks up behind me and wraps his arms around my waist, pressing his chest to my back.

We stand there for a moment in silence, taking it in.

"I've never been on this side of the stage before. I can only imagine what it's like with the crowd looking back at you." He says softly in my ear.

Our tour guide is giving us space and taking a phone call on the other side of the stage, so when Ford leans in to kiss my neck again, I tilt my head to the side.

"I froze my first time on stage with a large crowd. Singing in bars is one thing, but up on stage is another. The lights are bright and hot, and you can't see but a few rows deep, but you know they're there, and you hear them, and you feel them. Then, when they start singing along to your song that you worked so hard on... I had tears running down my face that night right there on stage in front of the crowd."

Then, Ford turns to kiss my cheeks, because I didn't realize I had tears running down my face. Holding me, he kisses the tears away, and it feels right.

"I can tell how much you love it." He says as we continue on with the tour.

As our tour ends, the place opens up to the public, and I can't help but smile back at the entrance. I will be there one day. I just know it.

"Where to next?" He asks, taking my hand.

"How about seeing Andrew Jackson's home?"

"Perfect."

The rest of the day, we spend taking in sights in Nashville. Ford is an undercover history fanatic, and seeing him standing in a president's home soaking up every bit of information, is fun.

As the sun starts to set, we decide what to do for dinner.

"My vote is room service and not to leave the room again until we have to catch our flight tomorrow." He runs his eyes over me hungrily.

"I can get on board with that."

Back at the hotel, I'm sitting on the bed, while Ford places our room service order. Thinking back, I can't get rid of this nagging feeling in my gut. It all centers around what Ford said at The Grand Ole Opry.

'I can tell how much you love it.'

I love what I do, but not how it's done. While I love performing for the fans and interacting with them, I hate all the politics of contracts, managers, and labels. Yet, I can't imagine not singing, nor can I imagine my life not here in Nashville.

So, when Ford joins me on the bed, I know it's time, to be honest with him.

"Do you know why I haven't dated, or even been with anyone in a long time?" I ask, wondering how much Lilly or Mike has told him.

"Well, I know you had a bad breakup, and I'm sure the touring keeps you busy," he says hesitantly.

"The breakup was the best part of that relationship. Then once I started touring and recording, I realized there was no way to keep a relationship, when I was gone nine months out of the year. There isn't a person in this world who would be okay with that, or even have that much trust."

Ford looks at me like he's trying to get a read on me, but I need to make him understand.

"I love touring and recording, so I gave up dating. I really wouldn't have had time for anything right now, if it weren't for this forced break."

"You're trying to push me away," Ford says.

It's a statement, not a question, and I turn to look at the other bed. I can't meet his eyes, because he's able to read me too well.

"Well, I'm going to prove myself to you, just you wait and see," he says.

I don't get to reply, because there's a knock on the door, and dinner is here.

Chapter 14
Ford

Mike asked me to come over to his place today and help fix one of the stall doors that was broken, while I was gone.

We got home yesterday, and even after our talk and the mind-blowing sex, Savannah still seemed skittish. Seems like now is the time to give her a bit of room. Lilly suggested the two of them go get pedicures at Megan's salon, so that leaves Mike and me alone today.

After we finish up here, we are both heading out to see Mac and find out what this Christmas surprise is he wants to set up for his family.

When I drive up to Mike's barn, he's already down there with everything that we should need.

"Hey, how was Nashville?" He asks like he hasn't already asked Savannah that exact same question.

"Started out really good. From what Savannah said, the meeting with the label went great.

We had a good time out exploring, but at the end, she put the wall back up."

"That's her ammo," Mike says. "She doesn't have to let anyone in. Because letting someone in, means she has to trust them, and she trusts no one."

"I picked up on that. Listen, I know she's your sister-in-law, but I want to make my intentions clear. I really like her, and well, stuff happened in Nashville." I pause, giving him a pointed look.

He nods, saying he knows what I mean without me having to say the words.

"I'm not going anywhere, but at the same time, I have no idea right now how to make this work, once she goes back on the road."

"You sure she's going to go back? She seems happy here." Mike says as he removes the only stall door from the hinges.

"Yeah, we toured The Grand Ole Opry. While we were there, we stood on the stage, and you should have seen the look on her face. The way she talked, she was so happy. I have to say she was in her element. Very clearly, she made it known to me how much she loves what she does, and there's no way she's giving that up."

"Doesn't mean my wife isn't hoping she will, and then end up settling down here with us. Lilly is trying all day, every day, to make Savannah fall in love with being here more than being on stage." Mike says as we line up the new stall door.

"Well, I wish her all the luck, because if anyone can, it's Lilly. She knows her best."

"Don't let her push you away. Push back. There hasn't been a guy yet who has pushed back. Well, that's her story, but it was before her singing days. Maybe, you should try throwing her off kilter and push back," Mike advises.

"Does this mean I have your blessing to go after her and date her?" I ask.

"You have always had my blessing. I wouldn't have let you go to Nashville together if you didn't. Besides Lilly and Riley's family, you are one of the people I trust most. Plus, I'd be more than happy to have you as my brother legally."

"Let's not get ahead of ourselves. I just need to figure out how to get her to not dump me when she goes back on tour."

· · · · ● · ● · · ·

Savannah

A relaxing pedicure with my sister is actually what I needed after Nashville. I've been hesitant to talk to Lilly about it, because Mike is always around, and I know he and Ford are friends.

I think Lilly sensed this because she suggested getting our nails done. The moment we got in the car, she locked the door and said one word that confirmed she knows I need this.

"Spill." Lilly orders, driving us towards the salon.

Starting at the top, I tell her about the flight there, the meeting, and our time out in Nashville afterward. Then, I relate what happened at lunch with Dallas and Austin, the light shows, and the amazing sex back in our room. I finish by telling her about the next day and the forgotten condom. Yeah, that's the kind of relationship my sister and I have, nothing is off-limits.

I continue on about our day out, what I told Ford when we were on the stage, and then our talk, before dinner, and the next one after. Finishing up, I tell her everything leading up to me reading the contract on the flight home, and him dropping me off at her place yesterday.

Rock Springs is so small that we arrived at the nail salon over thirty minutes ago, but we have been sitting in the parking lot for privacy, while I finished talking.

"You need a girl's night," she says.

"Isn't that kind of what we are doing now?" I ask.

"No. Megan, Riley, and their sisters do a girl's night once a month at the ranch. Because there are so many of them, and everyone is always busy, this is their catch uptime. Not only do they give out advice, but they keep secrets. What's shared at girl's night doesn't leave those walls."

Well, what do I have to lose at this point? The advice of over ten women I respect can't hurt, but maybe, it will even help.

Nodding, we enter the salon, and the moment we open the door, everyone quietens down. It's like all the customers are holding their breath to see how Megan reacts. When she turns and sees us, she squeals and runs over, giving me a big hug.

"I was hoping you'd stop by. Though I know you're busy, but we miss you at the ranch, both of you." Megan hugs us, and just like that, the salon comes back to life, and everyone is talking to us, asking questions, and wanting to say hi.

It's a good fifteen minutes before it calms down enough for us to make it to the nail area to get our pedicures.

"This place is what I call gossip central. Everyone comes here to chat. Megan hears everything, and some women make appointments just to stay in the loop."

"You make us sound so bad." One of the ladies getting her hair styled in the chair in front of us says. "We only talk to people we know. Remember last month that girl stopped in, and no one had seen her before. Never heard this place so quiet the whole time she was here."

"That's true. Any idea who she was?" Lilly asks.

"Nope, no one has seen her since. Megs suspects she came from Dallas, because of that award Anna Mae won, but normally, they make an appointment, so who knows."

It's then that Megan comes over, after finishing her client's hair.

"So, I have a favor, but you can totally say no," she says.

"Well, I came here to ask you a favor, so let's hear it."

Well, Megan says, "I have a girl who has worked the desk for the last few years. She just got her nail license over the summer, but she's still a senior in high school and needs the work. Not only is she excellent at what she does, but she also gives the most amazing foot massages. Are you okay with her doing your pedicures today?" She adds. "I'll make them half price." Lilly looks at me and gives a nod.

"Of course, we are okay with it, but I insist on paying full price," I say, and Megan smirks.

"Alright, let's hear your favor," she says.

"I hear you ladies have a girl's night at the ranch, and I need some advice." I chew my lips.

"About Ford?" She asks in a low voice, and I nod.

"We're having one this Friday, and you're welcome to join. When we nail down a time, I'll shoot Lilly a text."

After she leaves, a beautiful girl who looks barely eighteen comes up. Her eyes go wide when she sees me, but she recovers quickly and is very professional. I make a note to give her a large tip.

"Hey, girls. I'm Sam. Thank you so much for letting me take care of you today."

"We're here for a sister day, and this one needs to relax," Lilly says, pointing her thumb at me.

She gets started on Lilly's feet first, and then the lady from before, who is in the chair in front of me, looks at me in the mirror.

"So, how was your Nashville trip?" She asks, and I swear all eyes in the salon go to me, as everyone waits for me to answer.

Of course, they all know about it. So, I give them the G-rated cut version, leaving out anything complicated with Ford.

"The meeting went well. It's a lot to consider, but I can't talk about it right now, due to the contract clauses." I say, and they all nod.

"After the meeting, we went and toured Nashville." One lady joins in, talking about her visit to Nashville. How she made the Tennessee legends drive last year, starting at Graceland in Memphis, visiting Johnny Cash's grave and museum in Nashville, and then ending at Dollywood in Pigeon Forge.

The pedicure is one of the best I've ever had, and talking with the ladies, is fun. I can see why they come here just for the social aspect alone. All of the places I went to in Nashville were in and out. They didn't know you and didn't want to talk all that much.

The conversation in the salon goes on. I get asked about the band, and what really happened with all the press nonsense. They say how it's a blessing in disguise to be here with my family for the holidays, and I say I have to agree with them there.

They're genuinely interested in me, as they ask about the tour and life on the road. Many of the women sit in the waiting room after their appointment just to stay in the conversation. I don't want to leave either. I'm enjoying Mrs. Willow's storytelling, and Hunter popping in to see Megan on his lunch break.

For the first time in a long time, I feel like a part of a community; one that wants me there. While they're fascinated with my music and career, they don't seem to care one bit about what I can do for them.

Not once am I asked for an autograph, or for a favor for a family member or friend. I could get used to being here and getting treated like this.

That's when the warning bells go off in my head.

Chapter 15
Ford

Savannah is coming over for dinner tonight. She spent the day at the salon with her sister. We men around here know going to the salon is an all-day event, even if their actual appointment is only an hour.

It's a social gathering that lasts the entire day, and the men in town stay away. All except Megan's husband, Hunter, and his dad. His dad goes in to get his hair cut religiously. It started, when Megan and Hunter were dating, and his dad got involved and broke them up unknowingly.

To make it right, he came and apologized very publicly, while having Megan cut his hair. He's been going back ever since. Hunter stops in to see Megan every chance he gets.

Anna Mae is another stylist there, and her husband stops in from time to time, since his sister, Ella, also works there, but he's not there as often as Hunter. Thoughts of me showing up for lunch, if Savannah worked there, fill my head. I'd love nothing more.

But that's not our reality, and I need to focus on making this night perfect. I want her to fall in love with the ranch and see a future here. At least, for the foreseeable future.

Baby steps. We have to take baby steps, I remind myself.

There's a knock on the door, so I check on dinner again really quick, my mom's famous pot roast, and then head for the door.

My nerves increase with each step I take, and I try to ignore them and not let myself dwell on how important this is for me.

When I open the door, Savannah is there, and my heart skips a beat. She doesn't look like the rock star singer that the tabloids feature. Instead, she looks like she fits on a ranch. Wearing her skintight jeans and flannel shirt with her hair down, she looks perfect. Though, I notice her cowboy boots aren't new. They're used, and I wonder if she keeps them for when she visits here.

My dad always said a sign of a real cowboy is by the dust on his boots. The harder he works, the dirtier they will be.

"Hi." She says a bit shy while tucking some hair behind her ear.

"Hey, come on in." I hold the door for her to step inside. She looks around and sets her purse down on the table by the door.

"Whatever you're cooking smells really good." She smiles at me.

"It's my mom's slow cooker pot roast recipe. We have time before dinner, so I thought maybe, you'd like to go riding and see some of the property?"

"I'd like that."

I take her hand and lead her out the back door to the barn.

"This is Phantom, and he's my horse. Got him at sixteen from an abusive owner and worked with him for a long time to earn his trust back. He's now the best horse a guy could ask for." I tell her, as she pets him.

"This is who you will be riding." I nod to the horse next to Phantom. "His name is Casanova, and he's a real flirt, hence how he got his name."

That's when Casanova turns on the charm and starts rubbing his head against Savannah's like he's hugging her.

"You weren't kidding," she laughs.

"He loves female riders like my mom and sister, but can't stand any males riding him, even me or my dad."

She turns back to Casanova and rubs between his eyes.

"We are going to have a good ride, aren't we boy?" As she talks to him, he swings his head up and down, almost like he's saying yes and answering her question.

Laughing at his antics, we mount our horses and start our ride.

"It's been a while since I've had time to go riding. I used to love it growing up. I felt so free up here."

"Brice and I used to spend hours out riding and talking. We'd race, and then play cowboys and Indians, or cops and bandits on the backs of our horses."

"And you grew up on this ranch?"

"Yeah, my grandfather, his parents, my great grandparents, died really young and left him some decent money. He bought this ranch in a foreclosure auction and busted his butt to turn it around. By year two, he was making money again. Things got so busy he hired a housekeeper, and then a cook who he later married."

"That's so sweet." She says with a faraway look on her face.

"My dad and his brother were born on this ranch, but his brother hated small-towns and moved to New York City. So, my dad got the ranch. One of the ranch hands was a single father whose wife just passed away, and my mom was his. When my dad saw his daughter, my mom, and a senior in high school, he hired him on the spot and gave them both a place to stay. The way my dad tells it, seeing her for the first time, it was love at first sight."

"This ranch seems to have a matchmaking tendency, much like Riley and Lilly," she chuckles.

"My sister met her husband as a ranch hand here as well. They moved away a few years ago. Though she never wanted to run a ranch, she likes to help out. She helped set up our bookkeeping online and will come and lend a hand if needed."

"Did you always want to run the ranch?"

"For as long as I can remember. My dad started telling us when we were younger, the stories of the land and our family. I just knew I wanted my kids to grow up on this land as I did. When I was sixteen, my dad put me on the payroll as a ranch hand, and I started at the bottom and learned every job on the ranch thoroughly, even though I had been doing most of them already. My dad said I had to be willing to do what I asked the men who worked for me to do."

"Yes," Savannah says. "That's how I feel. I'm always right there on tour helping set up and break down as needed. There are a lot of people in the background, who allow me to be able to do what I do, and I don't ever want them to feel like I don't see them."

This doesn't surprise me at all. Just the little time I've spent with her, I can tell she's that way. She always left big tips, was the first one to help someone who dropped something, and she took the time to talk to any fan that approached her.

We ride out to the closest pasture with cows. During the winter, we keep them close. Unless like last year, there's a lot of snow, and then we bring them to the pasture by the barn, so they are easier to check on.

Taking some time, we sit at the fence, watching the cows eat some hay the guy put down the other day. Then, like she has snapped out of a daydream, she turns to me with a mischievous smile on her face.

"Race you back to the barn." She doesn't even give me a chance to answer before she's turning her horse and taking off at a gallop.

I laugh and follow her. The more she laughs, the more determined Casanova gets to win the race, and that's when I know she has already won him over, just like she has me. I just hope we can win her over, too.

The whole time we spend brushing down the horses, we are talking and flirting. It's nice to hear her so carefree, laughing and smiling.

She takes my hand, as we walk back to the house, and I pull her to my side.

"You looked good out there relaxed like you belong."

"I felt good. It's a freedom I hadn't felt in so long."

Inside, she helps set the table, as I finish up with dinner. Mom's pot roast recipe never fails, and it's still one of my favorite things she made growing up.

"Every Sunday, we'd have a big meal. No matter what was going on, all four of us had to be at dinner every Sunday. No work, school, or friends, and it didn't matter if you were sick, you were expected at Sunday dinner. This one is my favorite Sunday dinner meal."

"It smells delicious. But then again, everything that isn't fast food does, so I bet it will taste as good."

We dig in, and after one bite, she closes her eyes and moans. That low groan she makes, well, I swear it goes straight to my cock. He's at attention and upset she isn't making that sound for us.

"This is the best meal I've had since I was home last Christmas."

We finish dinner, talking about Christmas traditions and favorite Christmas memories.

"Want to watch a movie?" I nod towards my large sectional couch and TV.

"Yeah, a Christmas movie." She helps me with the few dishes there are to clean before we settle on the couch to see what's on.

We settle on *Home Alone,* and she snuggles up to me. I pull a blanket from the back of the couch over us and hold her, praying for many more nights like this.

But girl's night is coming, and lord only knows where that will lead.

Chapter 16
Savannah

Pulling up to the ranch with Lilly, I'm once again overwhelmed by its size. I know it's the second biggest ranch in the state of Texas, but I don't think you can fully understand that until you are standing here.

I'm outside, and I can already hear the laughter and shrieks of excitement, and smell the food being cooked.

It looks like Lilly and I are the last to arrive, but that's my fault because I didn't know what to wear. This is my first girl's night, and not just here, but any kind of girl's night ever. When you are so focused on your career, it's hard to make friends.

Like she can sense my thoughts going down a not so great path, Lilly walks over and hooks her arm in mine, and we head to the house together. We are greeted with laughter, the smell of sugar cookies, tacos, and tequila.

I've heard rumors about the girl's nights from Lilly. They seem to have a lot of fun and get into plenty of trouble, too. We don't get but two steps in the door, before we are surrounded by everyone, welcoming both of us. I actually feel like I belong.

Riley is at our side in an instant with her daughter, who we all call baby Lilly. She named her daughter after Lilly because Lilly saved her life one night when she was still a truck driver. She picked Riley up as a hitchhiker and got her away from an abusive relationship. They ended up here, and then Riley met Blaze, and they were the first of the bunch to get married.

"Look how big you are! It's only been a week since I saw you last!" Lilly says, taking the little girl from Riley.

"She hit a growth spurt for sure." Riley beams at her daughter.

"I can't believe she's going to be a year old in just a few days," Sage says.

"There's a party here next weekend. All of you will be there, even you Savannah," Riley says like she knew I thought the invitation wasn't for me.

I nod and try to smile around the emotion that has tried to overtake me. That's when Megan appears at my side.

"You made Sam's year with that tip you gave her," Megan says, studying me.

"I remember what it was like just starting out, not always having money, so I like to pay it forward. She's a good kid and deserves a break. When she mentioned it's just her and her mom, I knew paying for school wouldn't be easy." I try to shrug it off.

"Well, it was the talk at the shop all day today, and Sam hasn't stopped smiling. Now, get ready for some fun tonight. Everyone is already at least one drink in. Those of us that can drink, anyway." Megan says, and Anna Mae shoots her a glare and rubs her pregnant belly.

She pulls me to the kitchen island and makes me a margarita, while she keeps talking.

"The men are at my parents' place on the other side of the ranch having guy's night and doing whatever guys do. Playing cards, beating their chests, I don't know," Megan giggles.

"Well, I made them a batch of my brownies, so between the alcohol and the sugar coma, they'll stay out of our hair." Helen, Megan's mom, says.

"Okay, time to eat!" Maggie calls from the kitchen. "Ella just texted me she's feeding the baby upstairs and will be down soon, so she said for us to get started."

Ella is Maggie's sister, and since Ella married into the family, they took her brother and sister into the fold as well. To say this family is all about family is an understatement.

The siblings all still live on the ranch and plan to stay and raise their kids here. Together, they run the ranch, and though Megan owns the beauty salon, and Jason owns the bar, they'll help out any time and still know every detail of the ranch.

This is the kind of family I want, and how I want my kids to grow up. I watch everyone file into the kitchen and fill their plates full of food, before taking a seat in the living room.

Extra chairs have been brought in and are not simple dining room chairs. These are comfortable sitting chairs, along with a huge bean bag chair that Riley and Sage are sharing.

"Okay, Ella just texted again. She says to eat up because she's going to make her peppermint hot chocolate for dessert," Maggie says, and everyone cheers.

"Just wait, you will never want to have regular hot chocolate again," Lilly says to me, just as Ella comes downstairs with a sleeping baby J.J. in her arms.

"Who did you decide gets to hold J.J. first?" She asks.

"Grandma, who else?" Maria, Ella's mom, says standing up and taking the sleeping baby, so her daughter can go eat.

When she sits down, she more collapses than sits.

"Okay, what did I miss?" Ella asks.

"Nothing really. So, who wants to start?" Megan says.

"I will." Ella jumps right in. "Why didn't any of you jerks tell me about cracked nipples? He sucks so hard I bleed. What am I supposed to do?"

When I look at Lilly, we both smile.

"I told you nothing is off limits tonight, and everything stays here. They won't gossip."

The night continues with baby talk, news around the ranch, work, and catching up on everyday life.

"Before the night goes any further, I've had three of you ask why I'm not drinking," Sage says, and Helen's eyes jerk to her.

"Are you..." Helen trails off, emotion already in her voice.

"Ready to be a grandma again, Mom?" She says, and the whole room erupts into cheers and then quietens as soon as J.J. starts fussing.

Helen and Sage are still hugging, while Helen is visibly crying.

"Mom, I hope those are happy tears," Sage pulls back.

Helen nods and tries to wipe them away.

"With everything you have been through with your birth family, and Colt with his, I was worried you two might not have kids, but I didn't want to bring it up. I just want you both to be happy," she says.

"Mom, we want kids and lots of them. We just wanted to enjoy a bit of time together, after all the years apart. Remember, my dream was always to fill this house with love and laughter."

"Look around, dear. You have done that." At Helen's words, Sage looks around at all of us.

"I have, haven't I?" She says.

Everyone takes turns hugging and congratulating Sage, myself included. When I sit back down this time, Megan is beside me.

"You don't have to talk, but if you want to, we will all listen." She says softly.

"Well, I have more news that's a bit intriguing," Sage says, as we all sit down again.

"When I was in town last week, Kelli approached me. She apologized for everything. Sincerely apologized. So, we went and had lunch, and then talked quite a while."

"Who is Kelli?" I ask.

"She's the town slut who broke up Colt and Sage. That's the short answer, anyway." Megan says, not too happy before she turns back to Sage. "What could she possibly have said that made you agree to have lunch with her?"

"Apparently, she's been working with Miles to help with the possible illegal rodeo in the area. I guess several new ranch hands showed up; tight lipped on where they worked and all. Kelli did what she does best and seduced them for information. She says she got some stuff to help Miles, but she can't share it just yet."

The room is quiet, and everyone looks at Megan.

"Even if she did a nice thing, doesn't mean I have to like her. She went after my sister, has made moves on each of my brothers, and made my life hell in high school," Megan shrugs.

"I know, Megan. But there was something in her voice. She's different, and I'm willing to give her another chance, because I know there's no way she can get between Colt and me again," Sage says.

"Even I can see how much that man loves you. You won't be getting away too easy." I say without thinking.

Sage's face softens with a goofy smile, and then Megan elbows me again.

"Ouch!" I say to her, and everyone looks at me.

"I guess that's my cue to talk," I grumble, not ready.

"Maybe, I should start at the beginning," I say and launch into my story.

"I loved being on tour and singing every night. Not too much the politics and waking up in a new town every morning, and certainly, not the tour bus. But the lead singer's wife toured with them, and it was nice to have another girl on the tour. We would have girl's nights on the bus, paint our nails, and vent about the guys, the tour all of it. I thought she was a real friend."

You know, I should have known better. Even other people in the business still want something from you or to tear you down. I've seen it enough.

"Then, one photograph at the right angle was taken. It didn't matter that she walked out of the door a second after, or that she was there with us. It didn't matter everything we had been through together. According to my manager, *she* was the one who wanted me off the tour and pushed the band."

"What can she gain from that?" Sarah, Mac's wife, asks. Mac is Megan's youngest brother.

"Maybe, the husband said something to her, and she got jealous?" Maggie says.

"I thought about that. So, my manager sends me here. Then, my sister sets me up on that disastrous blind date, only for me to be rescued by Ford."

As much as I try to stop it, I still smile at his name.

"He hasn't pushed, but he just... fits, I guess. He kissed me after the concert, and I didn't even think twice, because it just felt right. Then, when I got the call to go to Nashville, I had this urge to show him Nashville and Christmas, and by the time I thought about the fact that I asked him to go with me, and how crazy it was, we were already on the plane."

"We were all shocked he went with you. He has been working his butt off on that ranch since his parents retired." Lilly chimes in and heads all around nod.

"We had sex in Nashville." I blurt out and bury my face in my hands.

There are squeals and giggles all over the room, though from here, I can tell none of them are Lilly's. She has a soft smile on her face, but she's still pretty reserved.

"And since you have been back?" Riley asks.

"I went to his ranch, and he showed me around. We went horseback riding, and for the first time in a long time, I felt free and like my old unstressed self."

"So, what's the problem we need to focus on?" Helen asks.

"There are several. The biggest. His ranch and life are here in Rock Springs, and my life and work are in Nashville. The next is that I'm still obligated to this tour if they decide to bring me back. Dallas says he can help me break my contract. What they did was a breach of contract, and I can leave that label. But then, I have to decide what to do next. Whether it means another contract and one that's probably at least five years this time. And the last, it's only been a few weeks with me and Ford. Neither of us is going to give up our lives for someone after a few weeks."

"I did," Lilly says.

"But you knew Mike for a good year before. All of you did, and if you didn't grow up together like Sage, Megan, and Sarah, then you knew each other for a year or more, even just in passing. Riley didn't, but her situation was a bit unique, and it was still longer than this!"

"I knew Lilly was just a big a gossip as the rest of us!" Anna Mae laughs.

"How else am I going to convince her to move here, unless she feels like she knows everyone and everything?" Lilly finally relaxes.

Sarah, who has been quietly listening, speaks up, "Honestly, you don't know the answer right now, because there isn't one. But don't push him away, embrace it while you're here, and when the time is right, the answer will come to you. It did for all of us."

"It took Sage getting stabbed for Colt to come around," Megan says.

"Well, let's not go that far," I say.

"Mac thought he was letting me follow my dreams by staying away, but it wasn't until we really talked, that we realized it wasn't true. And Hunter stayed in the background until Megan finished school," Sarah says.

"Royce tried for a year, and when I kept saying no, he got me drunk and married me in Vegas." Anna Mae says with a huge smile.

"That's not quite how it happened," Maggie laughs.

"I was dating someone else when things really moved forward with Greg. It was the hardest decision of my life to change course from everything I worked so hard for, but it all kind of came together on its own. The job offers, school, and the people here," Abby says.

"Enjoy this time with him and see where it goes. The answer you're looking for might be there tomorrow, but you still have time," Helen says.

Time.

Every songwriter talks about it being the answer to everything from loss and heartbreak to happiness.

It's easier in theory.

Chapter 17

Ford

It's only been a few nights since Savannah was at girl's night, but she has spent every night with me in my bed. Going to sleep with her in my arms and waking up with her there, is something I wasn't expecting to crave.

She fits in at the ranch, and the guys here really seem to like her, too. When Savannah sees a need, or even when asked, she pitches in and helps. Like me she has a love for horses, and she's always asking questions and learning.

Last night, I walked into the house and was met by the most delicious smell of dinner cooking. She had snuck away on a phone call and then had gotten dinner going not just for us, but for the ranch hands, too.

I walked into the kitchen and found her with the biggest grin on her face, and the ranch hands were all smiles too for some home cooked food they didn't have to try to put together themselves.

Today, we are heading to baby Lilly's birthday party. She's turning one, and they invited everyone. Savannah has taken over the bathroom to get ready, and I went to check down at the barn to see, if the guys need anything, while we are gone. Of course, they don't this time, but I always check.

When I get back to the house, I figure a quick shower and change of clothes, and I'm ready to go. What I wasn't prepared for was my breath being stolen by the sight of Savannah getting ready in my bathroom. Her stuff is all over the counter mixed with mine, as she does her makeup, and it's such a small thing, yet, I'm hard as nails.

I love the sight, and it's something I'll never tire of seeing. Standing, I spend a few minutes in the doorway, soaking every detail in, before her eyes meet mine in the mirrors.

"I'm just going to take a quick shower and get dressed," I tell her, turning the shower on.

"I will be ready by the time you're done." Her eyes follow my every move, as I strip out of my clothes and step into the shower, closing the shower door behind me.

As I let the hot water flow over my neck and down my back, I can see where Savannah is. The glass is frosted, so I can't see the details, but I see her outline, her leaning over the counter closer to the mirror, and brushing her hair off her shoulder.

It's doing nothing to help my erection go down, and in fact, the more I watch her, the harder it seems to get. With a sigh, I turn the water ice cold and let it run down the front of me. Only it's not helping, so I try to think of ranch chores, while I soap up and rinse off. It helps, until I step out of the shower, and just like that, instant erection again.

The moment her eyes meet mine, I can tell she's thinking the same thing. With that cute, flirty dress she's in, it'll make things easy for me. As I walk up behind her, she sets her makeup down and watches me in the mirror.

"We are going to be a bit late," I tell her, moving her hair from her neck and placing a soft kiss there.

She nods, her eyes still on me. I run my hand up the outside of her thighs, pulling her dress up with me as I go, and she braces herself on the counter.

"Spread your legs," I order, and she does with no hesitation. "Good girl."

Reaching around the front of the skimpy lace panties she has on, I find them already soaking wet.

"Glad I wasn't the only one turned on during my shower," I smirk, pulling her panties to the side and thrusting into her from behind. She's so wet, that with one hard thrust, I'm balls deep in her. Her moan excites me even more.

I'm not gentle, as my thrusts pin her to the counter. She reaches up and places a hand on the mirror to brace herself, and I reach my hand over hers. I'm so worked up, I know I won't last long.

I move my hand down to her clit and start lightly playing with it in the way I know drives her crazy. When she throws her head back, I kiss her temple and then add more pressure to her clit.

It's enough that she starts coming all over my cock, and it sets off my orgasm, which feels like it's being ripped from me in a delicious, powerful surge.

As we catch out a breath, I pull out slowly and right her panties, giving them a firm pat.

"You will go to the party with my come still in you," I tell her before I head out to the bedroom to get dressed.

Even though I didn't think we were that late to the party, but by the time we pull up, it looks like the whole town is here. It's a good thing their house is huge.

No sooner are we out of the truck than Savannah tucks her hand into mine for the walk to the door. We use the side door like we do every other time we visit. I don't know anyone who uses the front door when they come over.

The side door opens into the kitchen, which is where everyone is, anyway.

It's no different today. Everyone is piled around the food.

"You made it!" Riley says, coming up to give us a hug. "Food is in here, presents are on the table in the living room, and the birthday girl is making her rounds as well. Be careful, because she's crawling, and a speed racer, so don't let her size fool you."

"Let's go put the gifts down, and then get some food," Savannah says,-

as she guides me into the living room, where there are people sitting everywhere talking.

"Savannah! Get some food and come over here." Lilly calls out, as we set our gifts down.

There are all sorts of food, from subs to sliders, taco dip, and all the things you see every Sunday at the church potluck.

We fill our plates and make our way back to the living room, where most of the guys have their girls on their laps to save space.

"Well, when in Rome," I sit down, and then pull Savannah onto my lap, careful of her plate.

This causes her to burst into giggles, and everyone shares a smile. She might not realize it, but I just publicly claimed her. Not that anyone in this room didn't already know about us.

We fall into an easy conversation with everyone as we eat until Riley and Blaze enter the room with baby Lilly on her daddy's hip.

"Now that she's full and bathed, I think she wants to open some gifts, while you all keep eating," Riley says.

"She isn't a baby anymore," Sage says. "We'll have to start calling her Little Lilly."

"As long as you don't start calling me Big Lilly," Lilly says and gets a few chuckles from around the room.

"We can call her Elle, short for L.L. or Little L."

"I like Little L, but she still will answer to Lilly," Riley says.

Everyone agrees, and they sit on the floor and open gift after gift. Lilly is writing down who gives what, and everyone is enthralled in what gifts the birthday girl gets. It's like a competition to see who one upped who.

With Savannah on my lap, I enjoy every moment. Wrapping my arms around her waist, I simply hold her close. I was always the guy at the events, wishing I had a girl on my lap, and not just any girl. Now, I'm the lucky guy with a beautiful woman in my arms.

"This one is from Ford," Riley says, as Little Lilly tears into the paper.

"Oh! We were just talking about doing this! It's a kit to make a garden stone with her handprints!" Riley says.

"I figured she was getting enough stuff that Mom and Dad could use a gift, too."

"Now Savannah's," Blaze says, as he hands a bag to Riley.

Savannah rests her head on my shoulder and watches.

When Riley helps with the box, she freezes at what's inside. "You didn't," Riley exclaims, as Blaze peeks over her shoulder.

"I always thought memories are better than gifts, and she's getting a ton of gifts today." Savannah shrugs.

"Well, what is it? We aren't mind readers here, you know." Mrs. Willow calls from across the room.

"A weekend at The Water Park and Lodge in Dallas."

"That girl is a fish. She'll love the water." Mrs. Willow nods in approval.

They finish up the last few gifts, and then Sage stands up.

"I think my gift tops them all, but it's not inside." She motions for everyone to follow her.

"Come on," Savannah takes my hand.

We follow everyone outside, and then all gather in front of the barn.

"Bring it out, Colt!" Sage calls, and a moment later, Colt appears with a small horse.

"You didn't!" Riley says.

"It's a miniature horse and won't get any bigger than this. She's at the right age to get started being around them and on them. I saw him at an auction last week and just knew he was perfect. We have plenty of kids joining the ranch that will all need to learn to ride," Sage says.

Little Lilly walks right up to the horse and gives him a hug, as cameras go off like crazy.

Back inside, Lilly joins us on the couch and starts talking about the last year, and the birthday gift of her being born in the blizzard, and then finding out they named the baby after her.

That leads to everyone talking about their favorite memories over birthday cake.

One day, I want this, and I want it at my place. To celebrate my kids' birthdays with all of our friends crowding the house, and then talking about our favorite memories.

With any luck, it will be with the girl sitting on my lap, even if I have no idea how to make that happen.

Chapter 18

Savannah

The night after the party, I decided to stay at Lilly's house. We were talking about old times and just wanted to keep the conversation going, so I went home with her.

We spent the night on the couch, sharing stories, and many of which Mike hadn't heard, which led to many laughs. Mike went to bed and let us have some time to ourselves, and we were up for another two hours before we turned in around one a.m.

It was good to have a night like that with Lilly. We used to stay up and do that all the time when we were growing up. Talking anything out, and then getting into trouble for being up way past our bedtimes.

I think it made our bond strong and allowed us to be friends more so than sisters.

Though I kind of expected to be able to sleep in, since Lilly also had a long night, so when someone throws open the curtains in my room, I assume it's Lilly.

"Did you sleep? We just went to bed," I groan.

"Nope, I slept on the plane," my mom's voice says.

I crack open an eye, and sure enough, my mom is standing there with a huge smile on her face. I turn over, and then stretch and groan.

"That was Lilly's response. If Mike hadn't warned me you two were up late talking, I might have been offended. Now, let's get going, because I'm making hot chocolate cinnamon rolls, and when they're gone, they're gone." Mom says, leaving my room.

Since Mom only makes her famous hot chocolate cinnamon rolls around Christmas, and it's been a few years, since I've had them, there's no way in hell I'm missing out.

I jump out of bed and don't even bother changing from my flannel pajamas. Though, I make sure I look presentable, before making my way to the kitchen, where thankfully, Mom has coffee already going.

"Of the two of you, I thought Lilly would be the first one out here," Mom says, as Dad stands from the kitchen island to give me a hug.

"Missed you, kid," he says, kissing the top of my head.

I wrap my arms around him and take in the comforting smell of home. It's a bit of sawdust and a bit of my mom's cooking. It's my dad's two favorite things, my mom's cooking and woodworking. Then, I go over to my mom and hug her next.

"How are you doing, Vanna? Really doing?" She asks.

"I wasn't so great when I got here, but the more time I'm here, the better I am. But coffee first." I head to the counter.

Then, I make coffee for me and Lilly, because I know she won't be too far behind because she's probably getting dressed.

When she walks out, I know I was right. Her hair may be pulled up into a messy bun, but she's in jeans and a t-shirt. I hand her the coffee I made, and we both lean on the counter and watch Mom flit around the kitchen.

"Can I hire you to cook for us every day, Mom?" Lilly asks though I can tell she is only half-joking.

"No, but give me some grandbabies, and I'll be over much more often and fill your freezer," Mom says, pointing the rolling pin at Lilly.

Mike walks in then and seeing the rolling pin being pointed at his wife, steps between Mom and Lilly, making us all laugh.

"What did I miss?" He asks.

Lilly fills him in, while Dad and I sit at the table that's already set. From the smell of it, the first batch will be ready any time. Mom will make a few more because we'll eat them throughout the day if there are any leftovers.

No matter how many she made in the past, they never lasted until the next day.

"Okay, first batch up," Mom announces, as we all sit down and dig in.

"Now Savannah, have you heard from the band? And what happened, during this Nashville trip? Do you have plans?" Mom rapid fires questions.

"I have not heard from the band or my manager, but that has allowed me to think, so I'm thankful for that. No, I don't have any set plans right now." I pause to eat a moment, while all eyes stay on me.

"Nashville was enlightening. I met Landon and Dallas from Highway 55, and they started a record label," I say.

"I heard about them. They settled down and wanted to turn around and help the next generation of singers."

"Exactly. They took a look at my contract, and my label is in violation over all this, and they will help me out of my contract, no strings attached. But then, I have to figure out my next step. I can sign with them, and they laid out some nice terms, and I even have a contract in my room to read. I just don't know what I want."

"Because of Ford?" Lilly asks.

Both of my parents look at each other, and then at me.

"Who's Ford?" Mom asks.

"Mike's friend. We have kind of been seeing each other since I've been here." I say and wait for my mom to squeal because she's always so excited when I say I'm seeing someone. My mom is grandbaby crazy. Only this time, there's nothing. Mom is just looking down at her plate.

"What?"

"Well, I never seem to say the right thing, when you say you're seeing someone, and you have a huge choice ahead."

"What do you want to say?" I ask.

"That I'm happy you found someone, but not to make all your life plans around him. If music is what you want, that's in Nashville, not here. But this is all stuff I'm sure you know."

"I do, and it's weighing on me. But right now, I'm enjoying my time. I don't have to make this choice just yet, so I'm going to wait it out."

"Well, can we meet him?" Dad asks.

I look over at Mike, not sure how to answer that.

"It doesn't hurt to ask him," Mike says. "I'm sure he will say yes."

We spend the rest of breakfast with Mike and Lilly; talking about the summer camp they are planning this summer, and the new ranch hand they hired. While they talk about the new repairs, the entire time my mind spins, and I contemplate what I would do, if I had to make a decision today. I keep coming up with the same thing. I don't know what I'd do.

After the third batch of cinnamon rolls, I go to my room and get ready to see Ford. I could do this over the phone, but it's such a big ask, that I want to do it in person. My parents had no objection to it, as they are going with Mike and Lilly to tour the barn and see the updates in the bunkhouse.

Once I'm dressed, I text Ford.

Me: You home?
Ford: Yep, finishing up morning chores.
Me: Mind if I stop over?
Ford: You never have to ask. Is everything okay?
Me: Yes. See you soon.

I grab the cinnamon rolls I snagged for Ford. I'm guessing as a bribe for him not turning me down.

Taking my time on the drive to Ford's ranch, as I think over what I want to say, and how I plan to ask him. I know this is a big step meeting the parents, and this could go one of two ways. If he isn't ready, then he'll say no and get really skittish, which makes my upcoming choice really easy.

The other option is he's going to do it, say yes, and things go great, confusing me even more.

Ford is Mike's friend, so more than likely, even if he isn't ready for this step in the relationship, he'll agree to go have dinner with his friend's parents.

When I pull up to the ranch, he's waiting for me on the front porch and is at my car door, before I even turn the car off. I walk right into his open arms, and all the anxiety regarding these questions is gone.

"My parents surprised us last night and got into town early. They want you to come over for dinner, after Lilly told them about us," I say with my head still buried in his chest, and his arms still around me. His arms tighten, and he takes a step back to look at me. As his eyes study me, he cups my cheek and leans in to kiss me. It's soft and much shorter than I'd like. But when he pulls back, he's the one that looks nervous, and I get this sinking feeling he's going to say no.

"I love you, Savannah. But I guess I haven't made that known very well if you aren't sure if you can just stop by, or if asking me to have dinner with your parents makes you this nervous. I'd love to have dinner with them, and you couldn't keep me away."

I stand there in shock. Does he love me? But it's only been a few weeks. It's then I realize I've been so confused, because of all the feelings

I've been experiencing. I love music, but I love Ford, too.

"I love you, too," I whisper, and then his lips are back on mine.

"Do I have time to take you inside and show you how much I love you?" He asks against my lips.

"I'm going to insist on it," I tell him.

Chapter 19
Ford

We made love twice before she passed out. Now, I get to lie here in my bed, holding my girl, and plan our future. That wasn't how I had wanted to tell her I was in love with her.

Heck, I only just realized it myself at the guy's game night. I hadn't said the words out loud, but it just felt right, like if I missed this moment, I wouldn't get another one to tell her, and then I'd always regret it.

I know there's still a lot to work out, but I will do anything to get her. To have this woman in my bed, and in my arms every night, I'd do just about anything. When I see the future, it's running the ranch together, and her helping out different charities. I'm sure there will be some travel, so I need to start making plans for that.

I want to have all my ducks in a row, so when she asks, I have answers.

She shifts closer to me, and I turn my thoughts back to the here and now. With her pressed up to my side, her leg thrown over my hips, it's so peaceful and trusting. I vow I will protect her now and always.

When I look back at her again, she hasn't moved, but her eyes are open and looking at me.

"Watching me sleep?" She asks.

"Always. I can't seem to take my eyes off of you." I tell her honestly, as I roll her over to her back and kiss her.

"I love you, Rock Star," I kiss her jawline to her ear.

"I love you too, Cowboy." She giggles, as I hit the ticklish spot under her ear.

"Ford, you here?" My mom's voice rings out, and Savannah tenses up, and just like that, the easy-going spirit I worked out of her the last few hours is gone.

"It's my mom," I tell her.

"I will be out in a minute, Mom. Don't come back here." I call out.

"Okay, I've got some groceries to put away. Take your time, dear. Your dad is already out at the barn."

"They were planning to come up next week. I guess they decided to surprise me. You ready to meet them, too?" I ask.

Her eyes are wide, and she looks a little scared but nods her head.

"Let me call Lilly. Maybe, they can come over tonight, and we can do this all at once?" I have a feeling it's more about wanting the support of her sister around than trying to make things easier. I'll give her that.

"Of course. My mom will love it. You take your time getting dressed and call Lilly, and then come join us, when you're ready, okay?" I kiss the tip of her nose.

She's still tense, so I lightly run my hands up her side and start tickling her, and she squeals, jumping out of bed.

"Off with you." She tosses my shirt at me with a wide smile on her face.

She gathers her clothes and heads into the bathroom with that smile still in place. I get dressed and go out to see my mom.

As I enter the kitchen, my mom looks behind me, and then whispers, "Is that her?"

On my last call to them, I had told my mom and dad all about Savannah. I should have known that meant they would move up their trip to see us sooner.

"Yes, and be nice. She wasn't expecting you. Her parents got into town last night, and we have plans to have dinner with them and her sister tonight. When she asks you and Dad to join, please say yes. She's already nervous enough to meet you." I whisper as I hug my mom.

"Of course, baby! We like Mike and Lilly." She looks over, as Savannah hesitantly rounds the corner in to the kitchen.

Walking to her side, I wrap my arm around her waist, hoping to give her some comfort.

"Mom, this is Savannah. Savannah, this is my mom."

"It's nice to meet you, Mrs..."

"Oh, dear. Call me Kay!" My mom rushes over to hug her.

"Her name is Karen, but with that having a not so nice meaning now, she has switched to being called Kay," I tell Savannah, and earn a side eye from my mom.

That's when my dad walks in, and the wink he shoots me lets me know they saw Savannah's car, and this was their plan to make sure we were dressed and ready. My parents are respectful of my space and my life ninety-five percent of the time.

"This is my dad, Frank. Dad, this is Savannah." I introduce them and another round of hugs.

"That horse you got from Mike is looking good. Still a bit skittish, but once he's trained, he'll be a good horse. Well done." Dad says to me when he hugs me.

"I, um," Savannah starts, and all eyes turn to her, as she looks at me.

"They already agreed to have dinner at Lilly's-," I tell her softly and relief washes over her face, followed by a happy smile.

"Lilly told me that I wasn't to come back unless you two agreed to dinner," she chuckles.

"That sounds like Lilly," Mom nods.

"Come on, let's go to the barn, and I can give you a proper tour, before we get ready to head over," I say, as we follow my parents out of the back door.

I wrap my arm around Savannah's waist, and my parents use the walk to hold hands and talk to her.

"Ford here has told us a bit about you, and of course, we read about the tour. Have you heard anything from the band?" Mom asks.

"Not a word, which I'm more okay with than I thought I would be. Did Ford tell you about my meeting in Nashville?" She asks.

"Only that you met with another label, and the meeting went well. Mostly, he talked about what you two saw there."

"Yeah, I'm not sure what I want to do, but I know I don't want to be with my current label anymore. Though, my next move is still up in the air. Probably, until after the first of the year," she says.

We haven't talked about this, and thoughts start racing through my mind. Almost like she can sense it, Savannah squeezes my hand in reassurance to indicate we have time, and we'll talk about this later.

"Has Ford shown you around the ranch?" Dad thankfully changes the subject.

"Yes, we've been horseback riding," Savannah says.

"She rode Casanova who, of course, took right to her," I grumble.

"We raced back to the barn, and I won." She smiles proudly.

After we spend some time in the barn with the horses and talking about the ranch, we get ready to head to Lilly and Mike's.

For the ride over to Lilly's, my parents ride separately, because Savannah needs the time across town to get her thoughts in order.

"Your parents seem really nice," she says.

"They are. Even though they'll stick their nose in and give their two cents, they have boundaries and want me happy. But they seem to really like you, too." I squeeze her hand, and she relaxes a bit.

Once we pull in though, she tenses right back up. Sitting and waiting for us in the cold on the porch, are her mom and dad. While her mom rushes right over, her dad sticks his head in the door, I'm sure to tell Mike and Lilly we are here.

"Is this him?" Her mom asks.

"No, this is Billy Bob, a hitchhiker I picked on the way here." She says with a straight face.

"Oh, you. Ford, it's nice to meet you. I'm Cammi, and this is my husband, Allen. We're Lilly and Savannah's parents." Her mom comes and gives me a hug.

Her dad walks up and says nothing, but does shake my hand.

"These are my parents, Kay and Frank. I have a sister too, Georgia, but she isn't here with us yet," I say.

"Oh, she won't be able to join us this year. I thought she would have called you," Mom says.

"Is she okay?"

"Oh, yes, she's pregnant! But her morning sickness is preventing her from traveling right now."

"I'm going to be an uncle," I say more to myself.

"Make sure you call her tomorrow. Around lunch is the best time to talk to her," Dad says.

Congratulations are shared, as we walk into the house and are taken over by the most amazing smell.

"Mom decided to do her meatloaf, and she's making five loaves to stock the freezer," Lilly says to Savannah with a fake smile on her face, and her eyebrows raised.

"My mom does the same, when she visits," I tell her.

"Maybe, we can help you too, because I don't need that much meatloaf," Lilly says.

"Happy to help. Just let me know, once they're gone." I wink, as Lilly heads to the kitchen with her mom and mine.

"I guess I should join the girls in the kitchen," Savannah says hesitatingly.

"Well, I'll join the men in the living room ready to answer all the questions," I say.

When she doesn't move right away, I hold her face up to mine.

"What is it?"

"I know your parents just got here, but would you be willing to stay tonight? My family always does game night, and I didn't sleep well the last night away from you," she whispers.

"You know what? I always have a bag in my car, and I have no plans of going to sleep without you tonight." I tell her.

That brings a smile to her face that I'm going to try and keep there as long as possible.

Chapter 20

Savannah

I don't even have to open my eyes to know it's Ford curled around me. His scent is enveloping me, and it's more comforting than any words could be.

His arm tightens around me, and he kisses the back of my neck. There's something to be said about a man who will kiss you, even when he thinks you're sleeping. It says a whole hell of a lot.

The loud whispers from the other room start--up, and that must be what woke us up. Opening my eyes, I see we're at Lilly's place. We were up quite late and just fell into bed last night.

I turn on my back and groan, as the whispers get louder.

"Maybe, another horse showed up," Ford's referring to the abandoned horses that have been left in town all summer.

"Let's get dressed and go find out," I say.

A few minutes later, we step into the living room, and I freeze. Lilly's living room is pretty large, but when you pack in this many people, it starts to get claustrophobic.

Standing in front of me is the band Three Stevens I was touring with. Their wives, my manager, many of the road crew, and some guys from the label. They are all looking at me, and while they seem to be talking, I don't hear any of it. I can't breathe.

Without thinking, I turn and make a run out the back door towards the barn. I run until my lungs feel like razor blades from the cold air and don't stop until I'm in the barn, where I collapse into one of the empty stalls.

A moment later, someone is kneeling beside me and pulling my jacket on me. Looking up, I'm thankful to find Ford, because really, I don't want to deal with anyone else right now.

"You ran out without a jacket on, and I don't want you to freeze," he says.

Once I have the jacket on, he goes to stand, but I grab his hand and pull him back to me. With his back to the stall, he sits down next to me.

"Are they going to follow me out here?" I rest my head on his shoulder.

"No, Mike and your dad won't let them."

"Why are they here?"

"I don't know rock stars, but I'm sure they have something to talk to you about."

"They don't even have a show near here. They should be in Virginia right now. At least, I think so."

Ford wraps an arm around my shoulder and pulls me into him.

"This sucks. I feel like our bubble burst, and yesterday, was such a great day," I sigh.

"It was the best day, but we can get that back. Let's go see what they want, okay?"

Taking a deep breath, I nod. Ford helps me up, and we take our time, heading back to the house. Neither of us is in a rush to hear what the band has to say.

When we step in the back door, everyone in the room freezes and looks at us. No one speaks, as if they're afraid just one word will send me running off again. Ford places his hand on my lower back, and it's enough reassurance for me to speak.

"What are you doing here?" I ask, not sure who to look at.

The lead singer, Steven, steps up, but one look at Ford and he stops in his tracks.

"We are really sorry for how..." he trails off, as my phone rings.

I look down, and it's Dallas from the label I met in Nashville. My gut says this isn't a coincidence. When Ford sees the caller ID, he nods, confirming my thoughts.

"I'm going to take this." I turn and step outside on the back porch, before answering.

"Hello?"

"We just saw and wanted to make sure you're okay," Dallas says.

"I'm not sure what you saw, but I'm guessing it has to do with why the band and part of the label are currently in my sister's living room."

"I'm texting you a link." Moments later, my phone dings.

I pull up the link, and my jaw hits the floor. Apparently, it got out what the band did to me, and the fans decided to take matters into their own hands. Previously sold-out shows had a record number of ticket returns and cancellations, and my most recent single shot to number 105 on the chart almost overnight.

"Holy shit," I say more to myself than anything.

"That's an understatement," Dallas says. "I know I said I didn't want to hear about the contract and all, until after the first of the year, but when we saw this, we wanted you to know we're here for you. This is the best possible spin you could get. The downside is your label will try to take advantage of it, so be on guard."

We talk for a few more minutes before I hang up and forward the link Dallas sent me to Lilly, Mike, Mom, Dad, and Ford. I give them a moment before I step inside.

This time it's my manager that steps up.

"We're so sorry for the way everything went down, and we realize we didn't handle this well." While my manager is talking, I'm glaring at the lead singer and his wife, the woman who I thought was my friend, but now, won't even look at me.

"I still don't understand why you're ambushing me at my family's ranch days before Christmas," I say with as little emotion as possible.

"We want you to come back to the tour as soon as possible." The lead singer says.

"Not until after the new year. That's what I was told, and that's what I made my plans around. Now, I have obligations here."

"We saw your little charity concert. It was a smart idea to keep your name out there." One of the record guys in a suit says.

I don't even dignify him with an answer.

"Vanna." Steven, the drummer, steps out from the back of the room. "Please, come back on tour. I know how much you were looking forward to the Christmas stops, and you can still make those."

I shake my head, and the man in the suit sighs and leans over to whisper to another guy in a suit, neither of which I know their names.

"Think about it," Steven urges. "You can join the tour again at any point, but we need to leave now." He says, as moments later, all the guys in suits are gone, along with a few of the tour managers.

"We need to head out and set up for the next show." One of the roadies says, and more people file out of the house, leaving just the band, and their wives, and my manager.

"Well, I'm making a French toast bake for breakfast, if y'all want to stay," Mom says, as she and Lilly go into the kitchen to get cooking.

"You are welcome to stay for breakfast," I say in a still flat tone.

This isn't my house, and if Lilly is willing to help cook for them, then so be it. While my mind is racing, I can at least show some hospitality.

"Excuse me," I leave to go back to my room.

Sitting on the edge of the bed, I try to wrap my head around everything that just happened. A moment later, Ford walks into my room, and he isn't too happy either.

"Why didn't you kick them out?" He asks.

"Because Mom already invited them, and this isn't my house. Regardless of what has happened, they are still technically my bosses. At least, until this is fixed. I've always believed you catch more flies with honey, instead of vinegar."

"You are going back on tour?" He asks.

It's such a simple question. They came in person to get me back on tour. Something that could have been done on the phone. It's the grand gesture, and I get that, but the answer isn't so easy.

I had it in my head that I was here, until at least New Year, because I had that long to figure things out with Ford.

Now, that time has been cut short by just over a week. I can't wrap my head around all of this and worry I'm still dreaming. Maybe, I'm more hungover than I thought from last night. This kind of thing just doesn't happen.

When I think about going back on tour with them, my stomach sours. Before my visit here to Rock Springs, that tour is all I wanted. I loved every minute of it, even when I hated it. But there was still nowhere else I'd rather be. However, that couldn't be further from the truth now.

I don't want to go back on tour, but I'm not ready to give up my career yet either. So where does that leave me?

I look over at Ford, who is still waiting for an answer, and all I can think is where does that leave *us*?

Chapter 21
Ford

Pulling into my ranch, I finally take a deep breath. I stop at the gate and look at the house down the drive and the barn beyond it. I have never felt as crowded as I did spending the morning with the band.

If there was ever any doubt that I don't fit into the rock world, that's now gone. Even with them here in my town, it was too much. They aren't the kind of people I like to be around, and they are such a night and day difference from Savannah.

Even Savannah seems different around them. She was guarded, yes, and I can't blame her for that, but she was unlike herself. I guess maybe it was the rock star version of her.

Driving past the house and straight to the barn, I don't say a word to the ranch hands. I just pick up a shovel and start mucking out stalls. They all have been with me long enough to know I do this when something is on my mind, so they let me be and give me my space.

Only today, I'm not able to work through anything. I have a million questions on my mind and no answer for any of them. Why did she let the band stay? Does she plan to go back, and what happens after the first of the year?

Right now, she has them in the palm of her hand and can negotiate just about anything. Isn't that where any singer wants to be? If she goes back, she will get exactly what she wants. And if she goes back, then where does that leave us?

My dad steps up beside me and just stands there, leaning on the gate. He doesn't say a word, watching me. After a moment I stop, and it all comes pouring out of me. Everything that has happened from the moment I opened my eyes this morning.

"Well, it sounds like you both have some tough choices to make," Dad says.

"Not me, her," I grunt and continue on to the last stall.

"Not just her. What do you want? Do you want her? Have you told her that? Are you willing to follow her on tour, or do you want her to stay here with you? Have you talked about it with her?"

"Thanks, Dad. You just added to the growing pile of questions I can't answer right now."

He chuckles then. "You know your mom has an amazing singing voice."

I pause and look at him. "I know she does, because she used to sing us to sleep all the time, and I would love to come in the house and hear her singing in the kitchen," I say.

"When we were dating, she would sing anywhere she could. Dive bars, street corners, and charity events. One of those events caught a record guy's ear. He brought her out to Nashville, wined and dined her, and offered her a generous contract."

"I never knew this." I shake my head.

"Well, I almost lost her, because I assumed she wanted the contract so badly, that I was going to step back, and let her sign it, and let her live her dreams. We stood in that driveway there." He points back towards the house.

"She had the contract in her hand, and I was going to let her get in the car and drive away. My heart was breaking, but I thought it's what would make her happy. Then, she got in the car, started it, and drove down the drive and away. I turned to come out here to the barn and only made it a few steps, before she drove back up, jumped out of the car, and started yelling at me."

"I told him he was a damn fool for letting me go and giving up what we had, and how dare he push me into something I didn't want without even talking to me," Mom says, walking up next to Dad with a huge smile on her face.

"Then, she stomped right up to me and yelled in my face 'I love you, you idiot.' I dropped to one knee right then and there and asked her to marry me."

"I said yes and threw the contract in the trash and haven't regretted that decision once." Dad leans over and kisses Mom. Something I got used to growing up here was there was never a lack of love in the house, no matter how grossed out my sister and I got.

Mom and Dad head back to the house, and I start moving some hay around with more thoughts swirling through my head. This time, when I turn towards the barn doors, Savannah is standing there watching me.

A glance around shows that the ranch hands have cleared out. Smart guys.

"You barely said anything, before you left." She takes a step towards me.

"Not my thing. Plus, I had stuff to do around here," I say.

"It was pretty overwhelming having everyone there this morning. I didn't even know half those people, not anyone that was in a suit."

It's then I turn and fully look at her. She looks so at home here in the barn. Like she belongs on the ranch here with me, but she looked at home with the band, too. She fit in with them.

When I don't say anything, I watch her guard go back up. Before I can say a word, the wall is between us.

"I could tell something was wrong, and I wanted to come see if you were okay."

"Well, I heard you're planning to go back on tour. Good for you. I know that's what you wanted all along," I say.

"I never said that," she's looking at me like I'm crazy.

"You must have said it to your manager because he was on the phone bragging that he got you to come back on tour. I wish I had heard it from you, though." Then, I turn my back on her and start moving some hay around just to have something to do.

"Ford, I never agreed to go back on tour!"

"Well, you said something, because he was all over it! You should have just talked to me because now, I'm sitting here wondering what the fuck was I thinking? I thought we had something here. That I love you meant something," I yell.

"It did mean something to me, but if you are going to believe the words of a man who has shown he will lie, cheat, and steal to get what he wants over those of the one you claim to love. Then, what the hell am I even doing here? Was I just someone to warm your bed this Christmas? Someone to tell your future wife you nailed the rock star? Good for you, Ford." She turns and walks off back to the house without another word.

"Did any of this even mean anything to you?" I yell after her.

She stops walking but doesn't turn around. I wait for her to say anything. To give me any sign that any of this was real. Instead, she keeps walking back to her car.

What an idiot I've been. It isn't until the sun starts to set that my dad's story really begins to sink in. Not once, did I tell her I want her to stay, that I want her. All did was go off on her and give her every reason to leave.

So, how the hell do I fix this?

· · · ● · ● ● · ·

Savannah

Did any of this even mean anything to you?

Those words keep rolling through my head on the drive back to Lilly's house. I didn't answer him. How could I? All he was looking to do was hurt me, and nothing I said would have mattered right then.

Plus, not once did he say that what we had mattered to him, so it's a moot point.

That's what I keep trying to tell myself.

I knew something was wrong with Ford by the way he left Lilly's, but it took another hour before I could get the band to leave, promising I'd think about everything we talked about.

My only thought was to get to Ford and to talk to him because he'd been my rock through all of this. I knew if I could just get my thoughts out, he'd help me see the path I should take.

If I'm being honest, I just needed him to give me a reason to stay or a reason to go. He gave me the reason to go.

As I pull up in Lilly's driveway, I know what I have to do, even if my heart is aching at the thought.

"So, how did it go?" Mom asks, knowing I went to talk to Ford.

"Looks like I'm going back on tour," I turn and head straight for my room. I don't even get to the hallway before Lilly is in my path stopping me.

"What?" She asks.

"I'm going back on tour because he doesn't want me here."

"That's not true, and you know it." Lilly crosses her arms.

"He all but told me to go. He didn't give me any reason to stay, nor did he ask me to stay.

What's more, he made up his opinion from a conversation he overheard my manager have with someone on the phone and wouldn't listen to me. So, what's the point?" I raise my voice.

"Then, what was the whole point of all this? Leading Ford on, if you planned to go back on tour all along?" Lilly matches my tone, but the fire in her eyes is one I've seen only a few times before.

She's pissed, but I can guarantee she isn't as pissed as I am.

"Oh, take his side, because there was no way he was leading me on, so he could say he nailed the rock star that one Christmas. Then laugh and tell his kids one day."

"Oh, that's not Ford. You were finally opening up and letting someone in. The first chance you have to run, you're taking it. The band has proven they don't care about you, and yet, here you are running back to them." Lilly is now yelling.

Standing there looking at my sister, I wonder when she turned on me. She always had my back, but now, she has Ford's, and she has her mind made up that this is all my fault.

I don't say anything, but push past her to my room and start packing.

"Ford has done everything to show you how he feels. Yet, you're back in your old habits and running towards people you know don't care about you, because it's easier, and you won't get hurt. You don't give a damn who you're hurting around you!"

At this point, my back is towards Lilly, but the tears are running down my face, and I can't stop them. But I don't bother trying to talk, because I don't think I could. Thankfully, this is when my mom steps in.

"That's enough. As much as I agree with Lilly, this is still Savannah's choice to make, and we're her family, and we support her, right or wrong. You don't know the conversation she and Ford just had, because you never let her speak. We need to trust she's doing the right thing." Mom says, pulling Lilly from the room.

I close and lock the door and slump to the ground and cry. I don't know what the right thing is anymore, and I have no one to talk to about it, which makes it even worse.

Though I don't know how long I cry, it's when I don't have any more tears in me, I go to the bathroom and clean up. I make a few calls, grab pen and paper, and say my goodbyes.

I may not know what I want, but I do know I won't be able to figure it out here in Rock Springs.

Chapter 22

Ford

I didn't sleep well last night at all. I kept thinking about everything I should have said to Savannah and didn't. Then, I'd go over all the ways I was an idiot to let her walk away.

At one point around midnight, I was ready to go over there and talk to her, but my dad was up and told me we should both take the night and think. I needed to have a plan of what I want to say. He said this wasn't the time to wing it, and I know he's right.

So, I sat down at my desk and wrote out everything I wanted to tell her, and I went through so many drafts. Yet, nothing I wrote felt right. Then, as the sun started to rise, I knew what I wanted to say.

Getting up, I took a shower and made my way to Mike and Lilly's. Since they're up with the sun, I didn't think they'd be surprised to see me here, to be honest.

Going up the walk to the front door, I go over and over in my head one line that I know I want to say.

When Mike opens the door, he doesn't look like he got much sleep either. He also doesn't look so happy with me.

"What do you want, Ford?" He asks almost annoyed.

"Savannah and I had a fight. But I didn't say what I should have, and I want to talk to her to make it right. Mike, I have to make it right." I'm hoping that, if I'm brutally honest, he won't get in the way.

"Savannah left yesterday," Lilly says from behind Mike.

He steps back and lets me in.

"What do you mean left?"

"She was under the impression you wanted her to go back on tour, so she packed up and went," Lilly says.

In shock, I sit on the couch, shaking my head. No matter what happened yesterday, I didn't want her to leave.

"I never said that. When I heard her manager saying he got her to agree to go back on tour, and she hadn't told me, well, that's what we fought about. I never said I wanted her to go."

"But you didn't say you wanted her to stay either." Lilly's mom says.

"No, I didn't. That's what I came here to say today."

"Ford, this is what she does. It's easier to go back to the band, because she knows they don't care about her, so she isn't going to get hurt," Lilly says.

Her mom disappears and comes back a moment later with an envelope.

"She left this for you," then hands me the envelope with my name on the front.

I take it, but I'm not able to read it, not here, not now.

That's when the truck pulls up in the driveway, and I jump up with the hope that she came back, and we can still have time to work this out.

But it's not her. It's Royce and his wife, Anna Mae. Mike and Lilly meet them on the porch.

"Is Savannah here?" Anna Mae asks.

"No, she left yesterday," Lilly says.

"Did you know?" Anna Mae asks.

"Know what?"

"She bought us everything for the baby, down to two years of clothes."

"I knew she was your Secret Santa, but I didn't know she went all out," Lilly says.

I flip the letter over in my hands. How much of an idiot do you have to be to mess things up with a girl who is so selfless as to help out new parents in that manner, even before leaving town pissed at you.

I don't know what's in this letter, but as I stand there and listen to everyone talk, I just hope it's a ray of light or a hint on how I can fix this.

I say my quick goodbyes and head home. Locking myself in my room, I don't say good morning to Mom or Dad. I just lock the door and sit on the bed, looking at the letter. With shaky hands, I open it and start reading.

Ford,

I never wanted to leave this way, but I know now it's best that I do, for us both. We have the ability to tear each other apart, and I couldn't live with myself if I did that to you.

It was always the plan to go back on tour, but what I wanted started to get less and less clear the more time I spent with you.

Music has always been there for me. It's never let me down, and I can't imagine walking away from it. So, to hear you ever say I have to pick one would kill me.

As for what all this was, it was the best few weeks of my life. It was everything I always dreamed of, and everything I always wanted. I love you, Ford, with all my heart, and I always will, but there's no way for this to work out.

You are in Rock Springs. I'm in Nashville, and I have a tour to finish. I gave my word, and my fans are demanding it.

I will say thank you because you gave me inspiration and a reason to keep doing what I do.

But the sad truth is that Lilly and my mom keep reminding me this is what I do. I thought I was in love before, and I was so wrong. He nearly destroyed me. It was music that saved me, and I can't walk away from that.

I love you, Ford, but I have to do this.

Always Yours,

Savannah

Reading the letter over, I'm sure she meant it as a goodbye. But all I see is the reasons she's trying to remind herself that this won't work. My gut says this isn't over. My heart says it won't ever be over.

So, I pull out my phone and let *her* know, this isn't over.

Me: I love you, Savannah. Go out there and shine, just know I will always be here for you when you're ready. I'm yours.

• • • • • • • • • •

Savannah

It's Christmas Eve morning, and I thought I'd be over the moon for this part of the tour, but I've hated every day, and every minute of it.

I don't want to be here. Not anymore. Reaching for my phone, I read through the texts Ford has been sending me every day, and sometimes, several times a day since I left.

Ford: You did well on your interview Rock Star. But you looked a little tired. Try to get some sleep.

Ford: Good luck at your show tonight. I know this is one you have been looking forward,-too. I love you.

Ford: Good morning, Rock Star. I miss you, and I'm still yours.

That last one just came in, as I was reading the older ones. He's been following the tour, every interview, and show, and he hasn't been shy about it.

He texts how much he loves me several times a day, and there's always a good morning and a good night text, even if I haven't answered him.

I miss him like crazy, and I love him still, yet, I freeze every time I go to text him. Since I don't know what to say, or how to say it, then I don't say anything. Every day I wake up wondering if today is the day he won't text since he hasn't heard from me.

As much as I loved the tour previously, now my heart isn't in it anymore. I've been trying to figure out my next steps, and it's on my mind, as I get up and get dressed. Leaving the bus, I go to the back rooms of the stadium we're singing at tonight. This entire tour I've been walking around on autopilot. Then, it's like fate got tired of waiting on me to come to the conclusion I need to because right in front of me is a band poster of Highway 55 with Dallas and Landon.

I walk outside and down the sidewalk to call Dallas. If anyone would be a good sounding board, it would be him. They recently made the shift from touring to being home with their family.

We spend the next hour talking. He listens to what I want, and not once says it's stupid, or that I can't have it. In fact, he has a lot of great ideas to make it work. When we hang up the phone, I'm smiling, really smiling, for the first time, since I left Rock Springs.

Now, I have a plan. It doesn't involve getting on stage tonight, and that doesn't scare me. Instead, I feel free. Though, I have a few more things to take care of here. Heading back to the bus, I look for Dallas's email that has the last of the info I need, and sure enough, it's already waiting on me.

The next step is talking to my manager. I know he has a hotel room nearby, so I ask the bus driver for his room number and go right there, figuring it's best to get this over with.

When I knock on his door, the sounds coming from behind the door indicate he has company. All the better, if I interrupted him getting laid, he will want me out of here faster, and this might go over even better than I expected.

The problem is, when he opens the door there's no female to be seen, which means he's hiding someone.

"We need to talk," I push my way in.

"This can wait. I'm busy," he says.

"I noticed." I nod to the spiked heels on the floor by his bed.

"What is it?" He says, buttoning up his shirt.

"I'm done touring. I won't be at the show tonight."

"Like hell you won't; you're under contract."

"Yeah, you'll have an email about that. Seeing how you broke the contract several times this month alone, it won't hold up."

When I turn to leave, I spot a very familiar clutch by the door, and everything starts to make sense. This whole time, I was the scapegoat, trying to throw off suspicion. I whip out my phone and flip the video on to show the handbag, then turn towards the bathroom where I'm sure she's hiding.

Talking to my manager, I say with a gleam in my eye, "You're fucking the lead singer's wife! Then, you thought to ruin my career to cover your ass?"

"It would have worked if you had just kept quiet!" My former friend comes charging from the bathroom in nothing but a thin robe.

"Well, now your marriage and both your careers are over." I turn the video off and stride out of the door.

On the way back to the bus, I send Dallas the video and call him.

"Listen, I just sent you a video, but I don't want to use it if we don't have to," I tell him.

"Let me take a look. I've just got it," he says, as I hear some shuffling, and then my own voice, but a bit muffled.

"I agree with you," Dallas says. "Having this video will allow us to get our plan taken care of by the first of the year."

"That would be great. I'm going back to the bus to get my stuff now."

"Okay, you have a plane to catch. I just booked your tickets. Let me know when you get to the airport, so I know you are free of them. We'll see you soon."

Not a single person bothers me, as I pack my bags. I'm sure a massive text went out on my way from the hotel. I'm okay with that. After I say a few goodbyes, I catch a cab to the airport, finally free.

Free, but not quite done with my plans. It's going to be a long day, and it's not even lunchtime.

Chapter 23

Ford

I stare at my phone, as I eat lunch and finally pick it up and send Savannah another text.

Me: I'll be watching the live stream of your show tonight. I've already set aside the whole night. Miss you, Rock Star.

She hasn't responded once, but I'm not giving up. I know we just need to talk, and we can work this out. I don't have any doubts.

No matter how long it takes, I will keep trying, because I have no plans of going anywhere. I'm still hopeful one day she will let me apologize, and we can start moving forward no matter how slow it is.

A few hours later, I'm helping my dad put together a new desk for the office, so we can both work when he's here. My mom is in the kitchen making dinner. She has been cooking all day stocking not just my freezer, but the freezer down at the bunkhouse for the ranch hands.

Even though I know I would have heard it if it had gone off, I keep checking my phone.

"Still nothing from Savannah?" Dad asks.

When I got home from Lilly's the morning after Savannah left, I told my mom and dad everything. I was never so thankful they had planned to stick around, until New Years, because the last thing I wanted was to be alone right now.

"No, but I'm not giving up. You sure you okay to watch her show with me tonight?" I ask.

"We wouldn't miss it, baby," Mom steps into the room.

While my mom is with us, we talk about our plans for Christmas, which is tomorrow. Mike and Lilly invited us for Christmas dinner, and my mom accepted. She's going over early to help cook and have some girl time, while us guys are heading out to the barn.

I know it sounds like we are going to the barn to work on Christmas, but we really head out to drink whiskey, and shoot the shit, while we give the women space in the kitchen to talk about us.

As we start installing one of the legs on the desk, there's a knock at the door.

"You expecting anyone, son?" Dad asks.

"No, but this close to Christmas, it could be anyone stopping in to see you two," I get up and make my way to the door.

When I open it, I see the last person I was expecting, Savannah.

Without thinking, I pull her into a tight hug. I don't care why she's here, or even if she can't stay, I just need to hold her.

"Ford," she giggles but holds on to me just as tight.

Only when I loosen my grip and lean back enough to look into her eyes, does she speak.

"I'm so sorry for leaving the way I did. I should have..."

"No, I'm sorry," I say, cutting her off. "I shouldn't have snapped like that, and I should have told you I want you here and want you to stay as long as you want. If you need to tour, then do it, but I'd be here waiting for you, no matter what you decide to do."

Her eyes are misty, and she smiles big.

"I want to stay here."

Staring at her, I'm certain I misheard her.

"Through New Year's?" I ask hesitantly.

"No, for good. I've already talked to Dallas and worked it out." I don't let her finish, because I don't care what she has decided to do.

She wants to be here with me, and that's good enough for me. My lips land on hers, as I pull her into the house and close the door, pinning her to it.

"You're staying here with me. Move your stuff into my room. I don't want to spend another night without you," I whisper against her lips.

"I was hoping you'd say that. This was my first stop."

My lips barely have a chance to land on hers again, before my father is clearing his throat from behind us. With a groan, I break away from her.

Not even hiding from her how much she turns me on, I reach down and adjust myself. Then lead her into the living room, where my parents are.

Before sitting down next to me on the couch, she gives them each a hug.

"Are you back for the holiday?" Mom asks.

"If Ford will have me, I'm back for good." She looks up at me.

"Of course, I will." I lean down and give her another kiss.

"What about the tour?" Dad asks.

"I wasn't happy, and then today, it was like the universe was trying to get my attention. Everywhere I turned, there was Highway 55. So, I gave Dallas a call. I explained what I wanted, and he was more than willing to work with me."

"What would that be?" Mom asks.

"I want to still do my music, but not as I have been. I want to write for the love of it; not under a deadline to get the music out. Dallas asked about singing, and I said I'd like to do it to help charities and all, but I don't want to tour. So, he suggested I write songs for his label and give his artists first crack at them unless I wanted to record it myself. Then, he said if he didn't have anyone for the song, he'd help me sell it."

She turns to look at me then. "I agreed, and I can write anywhere. If I want to do a few shows a year and record a few songs, I'd be happy. Then, I could be home fifty weeks a year, and only gone for two, instead of the other way around."

When she calls this place home, the grin I'd been holding back takes over.

"If you need more time, I'm okay with that, too. I think a yearly trip to Nashville would be a great tradition to start." I tell her.

"While you guys are gone, we can come and oversee the ranch," Dad says.

"Tell me what you need. Do you want a place to write? We can build you a studio anywhere on the property, and if you want to still record music, then we can build a recording studio out here, too."

"Slow down, Cowboy. There's space in the Dallas' studio, where I can record and Landon has a friend who is more than willing to let us use his space," she says.

"And this is what you want?" I need to be sure.

"Well, there's one more detail we have to go over."

"Anything you want, and it's yours," I tell her, meaning it.

"I need to clear out my condo in Nashville and sell it. Know anyone who is willing to help me move?"

"As long as you're moving in here, I can get you half the town to help in a heartbeat."

"Well, I was hoping you'd want me here because it was getting kind of cramped at Lilly's. Plus, they get up way too early," she sighs.

"Have you seen them yet?" I ask.

"Nope, you were my first stop. Care to go with me to surprise them?"

"Of course. We could wait until tomorrow, as we're going over there for Christmas dinner." I tell her.

"They were going to watch the live stream, too. So, she'll hear, before then, when I don't show up to sing. I want to catch them, before then," she says.

"Go now, so you two can be back for dinner." Mom starts shooing us out of the door.

Once in the car, I have one more thing to tell her.

"Did you know my mom was offered a record deal when she met my dad?"

· · · · ● · ● · · ·

Savannah

We are just minutes away from Lilly's house, and I can't take my eyes off of Ford. It's so good to be back. I feel at home here, and my nerves are finally settled. Once I had made peace that even if Ford didn't want me, I was still moving here to be near Lilly.

But I was crazy to think Ford didn't want me. His reaction to seeing me at his door was more than I could ever have imagined. During the drive over, he has been constantly touching me, probably afraid if he moves his hand that I will disappear.

I have the same fear. Part of me wonders if I'm asleep on the plane and going to wake up and real life won't be this good. But then, when he parks and leans over to kiss me, I know life couldn't get any better. This is my new reality, and I don't have a single regret of walking away from the show tonight.

As we walk up to the front porch hand in hand, I don't bother knocking, instead I just peek my head in the front door.

"Honey, I'm home!" I call out, and there are squeals from the kitchen, and then I'm surrounded by Mom and Lilly in a hug so tight, that it's hard to breathe, but I don't try to move away.

"What about your show tonight? We were all set up to watch it," Mom says.

"Call in Dad and Mike, and I'll tell you everything."

A few minutes later, we're all in the living room, and I'm sitting on Ford's lap with his arms wrapped tightly around me, as I tell the same story I told his parents earlier.

"I can't believe they were using you as a scapegoat like that," Lilly says in a tone that I can tell she is angry for me.

"Dallas has the video, and I said I don't want to use it if we don't have to. He agreed, but simply having it is giving us the leverage we need to get this all done quickly and quietly."

"That's good. We should have Dallas and Landon and their wives out to the ranch sometime to say thank you for all this," Ford says.

"Well, I know Riley's family does a huge July 4th event every year, but I'd like to do something this year. I know it would be big and a lot of work..."

"Yes. You tell me what you need from me, and we will make it happen." Ford says with no hesitation.

"You know we will help, too," Lilly says.

"And we'll make it a point to be in town, too," Dad says.

"One more thing. I will be moving in with Ford." I look around, expecting some comment from my parents or even Lilly.

"That's good, because he sure as shit ain't moving in here," Mike says laughing.

"You are welcome to stay with us any time too," Ford says to my parents.

"I'm so happy for you two. I don't think I can remember the last time I've seen Vanna smile like this. Not even when she's on stage is she this happy." Mom says with tears in her eyes.

"So, we still on for dinner tomorrow?" Mike asks.

"We wouldn't miss it. My mom has been talking all day about what recipes to share," Ford says.

"I wouldn't miss it for the world," I say.

It's been almost five years since I've had Christmas dinner with my family. Five years too long, and I'm more than looking forward to it now.

"Oh, Anna Mae stopped by looking for you. She was in shock at all of the baby stuff you got her," Lilly says.

I try to shrug it off. "I got carried away. The baby stuff is just so damn cute."

"It's more than that, though," Lilly says softly.

"Well," I say. "They have been going through the renovation of that house, and I know construction isn't easy, and even more so when you are pregnant. I may have overheard the stress was causing some pregnancy issues. Hence why they went to stay at the lake house, and I wanted to help take the rest of the stress away."

Everyone in the house has a huge smile on their face, and it makes me a bit uncomfortable.

"Don't get too excited. I also volunteered you men to go help Royce put it all together. There's an entire nursery full of furniture he needs help with setting up."

I expect the smiles to fall, but they just get bigger.

I love this town so damn much.

Chapter 24

Ford

As the sun starts to rise, I know I won't get much more sleep. It's Christmas morning, and I have big plans. Last night when we got home, I took Savannah out to a cabin towards the back of the ranch, so I could have her to myself.

We stayed up making love all night until she finally passed out a few hours ago. Though, I couldn't take my eyes off her long enough to sleep. I drifted off at some point, but the moment the sun started peeking through the cabin, I was awake again.

The best present I could have is many more years of Christmas like this with my girl in my arms. In a few years, we might be woken up by our kids. They'd be running in and jumping on the bed, waking us up full of excitement that Santa came, and at all the gifts under the tree.

Until we go to the main house, it's just her and me, and I plan to make use of our privacy. Last night, I had asked my mom to bring a few things down to the cabin, before we got here. So now, I sneak out of bed and head to the kitchen to make my girl breakfast.

It's nothing fancy, just eggs, bacon, and coffee, but I wanted to be able to spoil her because I know the last few days on tour ran her ragged, even if she won't admit it. I can see it in her eyes, and the way the tension slowly eased out of her last night.

After I plate her breakfast and add it to the tray, I take it into the bedroom and freeze in the doorway. The sight in front of me is breathtaking.

The morning light is streaming over the bed, giving the white sheets almost an angel like glow. Savannah's dark hair is spread out on her pillow, and the sheets are bunched around her waist. She's lying on her side, and I have the perfect view of her beautiful breasts with her rosy nipples that I want to suck on. Breakfast be damned.

Setting the tray on the nightstand, I sit on the edge of the bed. The movement causes her to stir. She slowly opens her eyes, and when they land on me, her eyes light up, and she smiles.

"Merry Christmas, Rock Star," I lean in and kiss her.

"Merry Christmas, Cowboy." She sits up against the headboard, tucking her hair out of her face and making no attempt to cover up.

"I made you breakfast, but first, I have a gift I want you to open."

Then going to the closet, I pull out the medium size box that I had a put there last night after she fell asleep.

"I didn't get time to wrap it," I say, but before I can say anything else, her hand is reaching for the box.

She opens it and starts pulling stuff out with a confused look on her face.

In her hand is Whiskey's bill of sale, a copy of her most recent single, and when she pulls out a baby onesie, she looks at me.

"I am pregnant and don't know it?" She asks.

I laugh. "This is our life together. Whiskey is the horse that brought us together, the single for all the songs you want to record, and the onesie for when we start a family. Keep going." I nod towards the box.

She pulls out a leather-bound journal and tape recorder.

"For all the songs you will write."

Next, she pulls out a small American flag.

"For all the 4th of July parties you want to host."

Next is a Texas t-shirt.

"Because you are a Texan now."

The last thing she pulls out is the small velvet box that I placed at the very bottom.

"Ford." She gasps, as she opens it, and I slip to one knee on the floor.

"I want this life with you and any other part of it that decided to come our way. I want to spend it with you on the ranch, traveling to Nashville, and in our bed. I want it with you by my side. Will you marry me?"

I take the box and slip the ring on her finger ever so slowly. Once I place it there, she pulls me in for a kiss.

"Yes!"

Then, I'm on top of her kissing and sliding my boxers off.

"Your breakfast is going to get cold," I mumble, as an afterthought.

"I don't care. Make love to me, Cowboy."

• • • • ● • ● • • • •

Before heading to Mike and Lilly's, we stop at Riley and Blaze's. Pretty much the whole town will be in and out of the ranch today to say hello to them and get a tin of cookies the family makes.

Today is also the day Mac is revealing his surprise I have been helping him with, and he promised to wait until I was there, so I could watch.

The moment we pull up, his wife Sarah, is running over to my truck.

"It took you long enough! Now get in here, because I'm bursting at the seams!" She then turns and runs back to the door, where Mac is there, watching over her.

I take Savannah's hand and head inside. As the girls pull her in for hugs and the details of her being back, Mac gets me off to a side room to help finish getting set up.

This room is the playroom and soon to be schoolroom, once the kids are old enough. Over the last few weeks, Ford and I made a desk with each kid's name. There's one for baby Lilly, Riley, and Blaze's little girl, one for Willow, Megan and Hunter's little girl, one for J.J., Ella and Jason's little boy, and one for Sage's little one.

"Ready?" I ask him, and he nods.

As planned, I go out and call the family in.

"Mac and Sarah have one last gift for you if you will follow me," I say, and the whispers start, wondering what's going on. It's not often you're able to pull off a surprise in this family. There are too many, and someone always figures it out.

As soon as everyone enters the room, they notice the engraved desks.

"Oh, these are beautiful!" Riley says, running her fingers over Lilly's name.

"Wait, what's this?" Sage says, walking to the table in the center of the room.

On it are a few horseshoes, a pair of tiny cowboy boots, a onesie that says, 'new cowboy coming in August,' and an ultrasound photo.

Helen is the first one to the desk.

"Who is pregnant?" She looks around at her kids, and when no one answers, she picks up the ultrasound photo and reads the name.

"Sarah!" And a deafening cheer goes up, and everyone swarms Mac and Sarah with hugs and congratulations.

"I want a family like this," Savannah says next to me.

"Me too. We will make our family." I smile at her.

"We could start now..." she teases, pulling me from the room and out to the truck.

· · · ● · ● · ● · ·

We couldn't keep our hands off each other and were almost late to dinner at her sister's house today. Her mom spotted the ring when we were barely in the door. After our entrance, there were lots of cheers and hugs.

"I've always thought of you as family, but I guess it will be official soon, huh?" Mike says, standing beside me, watching the girls fuss over the ring.

"Yeah, you okay with that?"

"I wouldn't trust her with anyone else," Mike nods towards Savannah.

That means a lot to me, more than he knows.

While I miss my sister not being here, we video call her, and she gets to talk to Savannah and see the rings and talk with everyone promising to be here next year.

This certainly is a long way from the four of us growing up and celebrating Christmas. But our family is only going to get bigger.

As we sit down for dinner, the topics of conversation range from everyone in town, who the Secret Santa's were, to the company trying to get Jason to franchise WJ's.

"Riley said they are sending some big wig in from Dallas to talk to Jason and Nick about franchising the place. With all the publicity it gets thanks to Nick's cooking and the championships he's winning, they want to get in on the ground floor I guess." Lilly tells us.

"Well, if nothing else, it will be entertaining. Some guy in his five thousand dollar loafers, and fancy suit here in rock Springs, getting dust and cow shit on him. Bet the bar is full the day he shows up." My dad says, and we all laugh.

"In other news, Abby told me there has been a break in the illegal rodeo," Lilly says.

We all quiet down. The first horse was dropped off exactly one year ago today at the church. Black Diamond was starved, beaten, and drugged within an inch of her life. Mike and Lilly, with the help of Hunter and his dad, the town veterinarians, helped save her life.

Slowly, Mike and Lilly have earned her trust back, but she was the starter of almost a dozen horses left the same way the last year. One of the horses was pregnant.

While we have been lucky and only lost one of them, all the others have survived. It raised a lot of questions, like why they were being dropped off in Rock Springs, and why are they still alive?

The state troopers said normally these rings are full of gamblers, and when they are done with the horse that they have stolen, they shoot them and are found in a ditch, if at all.

There have been no leads, until recently Abby's husband, Greg, the town pastor, worked with the state troopers on a sting operation and caught one of the guys dropping the horses off. Unfortunately, they didn't learn much of anything from him, because he still isn't talking. All he says is he's following orders.

"What did they find out?" I ask.

"While the horses are being dropped off here, and apparently, the operation is in Dallas. It's not the normal illegal rodeo the cops thought it was. That's all they will say, as they don't want to leak too much and risk losing their lead," Lilly says.

"Didn't Sage say Kelli was working with them? I wonder if she was the one who uncovered this?" Savannah asks.

"Wait. Kelli was working with the state troopers?" Mike asks.

"Apparently, she was seducing some of the new ranch hands to see what they knew, but didn't say if she found anything out," Lilly confirms.

"Damn, that girl might have a sliver of good in her after all." My dad says.

My parents are no strangers to all the bullshit Kelli has pulled around town. From sleeping with married men, seducing truckers passing though, causing drama between Sage and Colt, and just being a downright mean bully. I don't think anyone expected her to lift a finger to help anyone.

"Well, here's to hoping they put this to rest soon." We all drink to that, before settling around the fireplace listening to Christmas music.

"Any plans for your anniversary?" I ask Mike.

Mike proposed on Christmas day last year, and they had a really quick wedding here on the ranch because they wanted to be married by the New Year.

"I have a plan, but it's a secret," Mike smirks at Lilly, who pretends to be annoyed.

"What about you sister? What are you thinking about your wedding?" Lilly asks.

Savannah looks at me.

"Whatever you want, I'm down for, just prefer it sooner rather than later," I tell her.

"I was thinking spring on the ranch. Lots of tents, inviting the whole town, Landon and Dallas, along with a few of my friends from Nashville, and asking everywhere to make a charity donation, instead of gifts. My dream would be for Landon and Dallas to perform for our first dance. It would be nice, if the vibe was relaxed, and everyone from the town enjoyed hanging out together for the day and having a good time."

"That's perfect," I tell her.

"Looks like we have some planning to do." The girls and their moms jump up and head down the hall. I'm sure they're getting online and looking at all the possibilities.

I couldn't imagine a better Christmas.

Epilogue

Brice

I'm leaving the diner with my regular caffeine boost of coffee in my hand when Savannah opens the door. Seeing I'm on my way out, and she holds the door open for me.

I tip my hat in thanks, wishing I could stay and talk to her, but I'm already late opening the doctor's office today. Without a doubt, I know my first patient will be waiting on me.

As I'm opening the lid of my coffee tumbler Jo just refilled for me, I bump into someone. Judging by the sky high heels she's wearing, she isn't from around here.

My eyes travel up her long, tan legs to the skirt and business suit jacket that shows a hint of cleavage. Her blonde hair is perfectly in place. In short, she's a city girl.

"You should get yourself a pair of boots. You will break an ankle around here in those things." I tell her, though I'm not sure why.

When people come in from the city, I've learned to avoid them, unless they come into my office. Normally, they come in with an injury that could have been avoided with the right clothes or footwear.

"Thanks, but I'm just in town to talk to the owners of WJ's." She points to the bar across the street. "Any idea when it opens?"

Everyone in town knows Jason and his chef, Nick, who own the bar. I don't know her, and no one inside will give her any information either. We don't talk to outsiders.

This is a rule I abide by as well, so I'm not sure why I say what I say next.

"Anytime now. Jason's wife cuts hair at the beauty salon. He likes to come in early with her, so he might be down there." I point behind her down the street.

"I'm happy to tell him you are looking for him, Miss..."

"Kayla." She says her name but offers nothing more.

"The diner here has some good food, while you wait for him," I suggest.

"No, this is business." She shakes her head, even as she looks through the window next to us.

The same window I'm sure half the downtown is watching our every move through.

"Okay, city girl. You be careful." I tip my head and walk over to my truck. Only when I open my truck door, do I look back to find her watching me.

I don't know why this girl caught my attention, but part of me hopes she's in town for a bit. She seems like she will be a lot of fun.

• • • ◦ ● ◦ ● • • •

Don't miss Brice and Kayla's story in **The Cowboy and His Billionaire!**

Want Dallas and Austin and more on Highway 55? Check out **She's Still The One** by Kaci Rose

• • • ◦ ● ◦ ● • • •

Make sure you get **your free Rock Springs Novella** as well!

https://www.kacirose.com/SageandColt

Connect with Kaci M. Rose

Kaci M. Rose writes steamy small town cowboys. She also writes under Kaci Rose and there she writes wounded military heroes, giant mountain men, sexy rock stars, and even more there. Connect with her below!

Website

Facebook

Kaci Rose Reader's Facebook Group

Goodreads

Book Bub

Join Kaci M. Rose's VIP List (Newsletter)

More Books by Kaci M. Rose

Rock Springs Texas Series

The Cowboy and His Runaway – Blaze and Riley

The Cowboy and His Best Friend – Sage and Colt

The Cowboy and His Obsession – Megan and Hunter

The Cowboy and His Sweetheart – Jason and Ella

The Cowboy and His Secret – Mac and Sarah

Rock Springs Weddings Novella

Rock Springs Box Set 1-5 + Bonus Content

Cowboys of Rock Springs

The Cowboy and His Mistletoe Kiss – Lilly and Mike

The Cowboy and His Valentine – Maggie and Nick

The Cowboy and His Vegas Wedding – Royce and Anna

The Cowboy and His Angel – Abby and Greg

The Cowboy and His Christmas Rockstar – Savannah and Ford

The Cowboy and His Billionaire – Brice and Kayla

Walker Lake, Texas

The Cowboy and His Beauty - Sky and Dash

About Kaci M Rose

Kaci M Rose writes cowboy, hot and steamy cowboys set in all town anywhere you can find a cowboy.

She enjoys horseback riding and attending a rodeo where is always looking for inspiration.

Kaci grew on a small farm/ranch in Florida where they raised cattle and an orange grove. She learned to ride a four-wheeler instead of a bike (and to this day still can't ride a bike) and was driving a tractor before she could drive a car.

Kaci prefers the country to the city to this day and is working to buy her own slice of land in the next year or two!
Kaci M Rose is the Cowboy Romance alter ego of Author Kaci Rose.

See all of Kaci Rose's Books here.

Please Leave a Review!

I love to hear from my readers! Please **head over to your favorite store and leave a review** of what you thought of this book!

55870273R00139